The Scent of a Man

By

Miriam Newman

Jae El Foster

Jennifer Patricia O'Keeffe

Kristi Ahlers

DCL Publications, LLC
www.thedarkcastlelords.net

DCL Publications, LLC

© 2021
Love Cabin by Miriam Newman
Exiled to Love by Jae El Foster
The Scent of a Man by Jennifer Patricia O'Keeffe
The Scent of You by Kristi Ahlers

First Edition February 2021

DCL Publications
1033 Plymouth Dr.
Grafton, OH 44044

ISBN 978-1-7362178-4-9

This is a work of fiction. Names, characters, places and incidents are the product of the author's imagination, and any resemblance to any actual persons, living or dead, events, or locales, is entirely coincidental.

Cover design by Jae El Foster

Cover model: Sylvester Bowden

Cover photo: Michael Van Truong

PUBLISHED IN THE UNITED STATES OF AMERICA

Table of Contents

Love Cabin

By

Miriam Newman

Chapter One

There was a black, furry lump on the roof. It wasn't moving. Peering at it from the second-story window of the cabin, Marjorie Cummings held her breath, watching to see if it was holding its breath, too.

She didn't think so. That thing looked...dead. In the year and a half she had lived here in her own little piece of heaven, she had taken a lot of things off that roof. Detritus thrown from a hot air balloon launched from her neighbor's pasture to give romantic tours to couples honeymooning at the nearby bed and breakfast. Birds' nests blown down in storms. Part of her chimney. But never—so far—anything that looked dead.

Oh, well, it was only a matter of time. She just hoped it wasn't what she thought it was as she prepared to scrape the skin off her knees crawling across the cedar shake roof. She had done a proper job of it last time, retrieving the nest to see if there was anything in it that she had to save. Restraining her impulse to crawl out, she grabbed a towel. If it wasn't what she thought it was, that could be a pad for her knees. If it was, it would be a shroud.

She was already crying. A divorce and having someone hit her newly-purchased car in the dealership parking lot just after she signed the papers hadn't reduced her to tears, but this promised to.

"Jack," she sobbed. "Oh, please don't be Jack." But she had never seen any wild animal, except maybe a skunk, that resembled a black and white tuxedo cat.

It was Jack—limp, topaz eyes still open, fixed on Kitty Heaven. He couldn't have been dead long. There wasn't a mark on him. It seemed as if he had been coming across the roof to the second story window where he had learned Marjorie would let him in if he meowed. Within sight of safety and cat chow, he had given up the ghost.

"Oh, no," she moaned. "Not you, too."

But it was. He hadn't been old, he hadn't been sick, and if he had been hit by a car there was no way he could have climbed the ginko tree and on to the roof. Was there? Guilt ate at her as she gathered him up, swaddling his twelve-pound body. She knew he was twelve pounds because he had just been to the vet for his shots. No matter how broke she was, Marjorie had always taken care of Jack. Her not-so-long-lost husband, Jeff, had resented it. She loved that damn cat more than she loved him, he had said.

She had thought he was kidding, until she came home unexpectedly and found him with Wendy the Witch. All the wives had referred to Wendy that way because she was newly single and on the prowl for men, with 80s Big Hair and cleavage down to there. Well, finally she had gotten one—Marjorie's—and, apparently, she meant to keep him, at least as long as she'd kept the last one. A few years with Wendy sent most men running for a divorce attorney, but Jeff didn't seem to have caught on, so Marjorie ran instead. Then it was just Marjorie and Jack.

Stumbling back through the hallway window, she skinned her knees bloody on the sill because she was wearing shorts that barely covered her butt cheeks. There was nobody who cared about her butt cheeks at present and it was hot, so she was leaving them free to the breeze. She wondered if Jack the black cat might have had a heat stroke. His fur was scorching to the touch.

Cradling him in her arms, she crept down the slippery steps to the first floor. There, she was forced to relinquish him to the couch while she located something sturdy enough for digging—no sneakers—and settled on Bean boots. They were especially fetching with short shorts, but no one would see her. Gulping a glass of water because she didn't want to risk heat stroke herself, she took Jack out the back door, pausing only long enough to lift a shovel from along the wall of the back kitchen. Chimney on the roof, bats in the attic, and a lovely jade-colored snake hunting mice in the kitchen had taught her to keep equipment handy. Her one and only next-door neighbor, an elderly widow, had died and the estate was being settled, so Marjorie was quite alone. Usually she enjoyed it, though this day she might have welcomed a little help. But that had ended the day she found Jeff doing bedroom gymnastics with Wendy the Witch.

Still, she would do her duty as always. She had no idea what had killed Jack and couldn't afford to find out. That would require a vet, costing money and changing nothing. Dead was dead. Over was over. Not yet thirty, she had already learned that lesson well. Stiffening her resolve, she hunted the yard for a spot. It was fenced in, ready for the dog she would love to have. She knew the silence in the cabin would unnerve her and Jack had clawed his way, expensively, through every one of her window screens to get out. A dog wouldn't do that. It might not come home to die.

Cat in one arm, shovel in the other, blinded by tears, she stumbled like a drunk around the yard, searching for a spot where there were no tree roots to block her digging. The ground was hard as a rock. Roots would only add to the job and she was already tired from cleaning the cabin on this, her day off. This was one hell of a vacation day.

"What are you doing?"

Marjorie jumped like she had been shot, totally unnerved by a voice coming from a place she had expected nothing to be. Frozen, she looked across her fence to the elderly widow's empty yard. Well, it was supposed to be empty.

Looking at her across the fence was a guy about her own age with hippie-length blond hair, an incongruous, neatly trimmed beard and very blue eyes. He looked like a Viking, and not a particularly friendly one.

"Oh...uh..." she stuttered, rattled. "I just...um...I have to bury my cat. He came home dead. Err...he came home, I found him dead." She knew she sounded like an idiot.

"Jack Calloway." He was obviously a man of few words. "I just bought Mrs. Clements's place."

Jack? He couldn't be a Jack. It was too weird.

"Uh, well, nice to meet you," she forced out, although she doubted it.

He looked at her scathingly: hair dripping sweat, no makeup, crotch-cutting shorts, bloody legs and Bean boots.

"You look like you got mugged."

She felt her hackles go up. "No, I was crawling on the roof to get my dead cat. Now if you'll excuse me, I have to bury him."

"You'll never even get the shovel in the ground." And then he walked away. Marjorie stared after him, wondering if she had ever felt more affronted. And this was going to be her neighbor.

Mentally filing Jack Calloway under "garbage," Marjorie had just resumed her search when the heard the creak of the unoiled gate on the other side of the yard and her new neighbor appeared. He had come on her property without permission. She looked at the shovel in her hand, wondering if she would need it.

He didn't give her the chance.

"Here," the Viking vision said, taking it out of her hand,

"before you hurt yourself."

Without another word, he stomped off several paces away to the only possible spot without roots. She watched as he sank the shovel in, one booted foot atop it. He was methodical, marking four corners and then digging from the middle, placing dirt across the imaginary line between corners so that it formed a neat, small rectangle as he dug his way to each mark.

"Is that how you do it?" she asked, feeling stupid.

"That's how I do it."

It did work. He was making impressive speed, although she could see sweat soaking the back of his khaki shirt. Her only contribution was to stand there helplessly with a dead cat in her arms.

Finally, he seemed satisfied, putting the shovel on the ground, standing in the hole.

"Whenever you're ready."

She wasn't, but Marjorie turned back a corner of the towel, assuring herself one more time that Jack the Cat was dead. But he really was dead. His coat shone in the sunlight, his snowy white bib and paws immaculate as always. Whatever had killed him had left no trace. He looked asleep, just with his eyes open.

What hadn't she lost, Marjorie wondered. Husband, home, car. Her place in life, her sense of direction. Now, she just worked to pay the bills and even the minor pleasure of coming home to her cat's pleased purring was gone. Giving him a last kiss, she covered him again, going to the edge of his little grave.

"Here," Jack Calloway offered. "You'll fall in."

He had dug the grave deep and she probably would. Reluctantly, she handed her bundle to him and he placed Jack the Cat midway in his final resting place.

"Do you want the towel?" he asked, but Marjorie shook her head. "OK, then." He stepped out, his long legs making it look easy. "Cover him up."

Apparently, that was the end of his offer. Silently, Marjorie picked up the shovel, covered Jack and tamped the soil neatly. She got the impression her neighbor was tapping one foot impatiently, although he wasn't.

"Cover it with stones so nothing digs him up," the other Jack advised. "You can take some from my stone wall."

"You're not going to keep it?" Marjorie was surprised. Mrs. Clements's place had been marked with old, probably historic stone walls that had undoubtedly fenced in cows at one time.

"I'm not much for walls."

"You want a hamburger?" she offered. She wouldn't take anything from this guy except as a trade.

He looked at her assessingly again, in a way that made her conscious of every one of her deficits. "No thanks. You look like you need the food."

Without another word, he left the way he had come in. Across the yard, she could see him bang his way in the front door where she had always been welcome, past the careful plantings and hummingbird feeders Mrs. Clements had hung with such care on the porch. She bet those wouldn't last long.

Promptly one hour later, freshly showered and wearing something that covered her butt cheeks, with bandaids on both knees, Marjorie went over, pushing a wheelbarrow. There was no sign of the new neighbor, but she knew her way to the stone wall. He was right that something would dig Jack up. They had foxes and coyotes in the neighborhood that wouldn't hesitate to rob a fresh grave.

If she got a dog, she thought, it couldn't be a foo-foo dog. Probably a pit bull would be a smarter choice. She might need one, with a jerk living next door. He was insulting. What did he mean— she looked like she needed the food? She didn't need a training bra. She had slender hips—so what? And great legs, although granted they had been bloody. He had certainly seen enough of them.

She had put on makeup that might not melt and managed to impart a faint curl at the ends of her chestnut-brown hair through judicious use of a curling iron. It was hot work in the heat, but she went nowhere without at least an attempt to do something with her straight-as-a-string hair...not even where an idiot now lived.

The idiot was nowhere to be seen. A light went on in the kitchen as dusk fell and she hurried to get the last rocks in her wheelbarrow. With her luck, Jack Calloway was a good shot and would say he thought she was a predator. Finishing, she pushed her load back through his yard and then hers, upending the wheelbarrow on the grave and piling stones until the mound suited her. Wile-E-Coyote should have a tough time digging through that.

And then, because she had to go to work in the morning, she showered again, turned on the bedroom window unit so that she couldn't hear anything and went to sleep under its cool vent, missing the soft lump against her leg that had been Jack the Cat.

Chapter Two

"You've got a kid in your office who thinks he'll achieve world peace by amputating his toe and letting his neurons flood the world," Karen warned.

Marjorie looked at the receptionist skeptically, trying to ascertain if she was kidding. Let her, just for once, be kidding. The younger girl shook her head.

"Bob took a pen knife off him."

"Great," Marjorie muttered. "Any bullet holes in the windows?" They were a treatment center for special needs and emotionally disturbed children, but people sometimes seemed to mistake them for a target.

Karen shook her head again. "Not so far."

It was only Tuesday and she had a dead cat, an ignorant jerk for a neighbor, a probably schizophrenic kid in her social work office and a headache. Already. She longed for coffee, but the last time she had delayed to get a cup, the client in her office had set her curtains on fire and they'd had to evacuate the entire building. Some people just hated to be kept waiting.

"I'll bring you some," Karen said, never looking up from her monitor. "Two sugars and cream?"

"Right," Marjorie said. "I love you."

"I know."

The rest of the day went as it usually went: an evaluation of an incoming student whose appalling history of abuse she recorded in every gruesome detail, a stack of files with the most urgent cases on top, an endless stream of phone calls and letters begging them to admit students, some of whom were far too disturbed for their program and others who were not disturbed enough—dump jobs. A mother who screamed at her that they had taken too long to evaluate her son and invited her to jump off a bridge. More coffee. Lunch at her desk. The dreaded intercom buzzer from Karen and her cheery, "Can you take an inquiry?" If she got a dog, she thought, it was going to need doggie day care. Jack had been a lot less trouble.

Jack. Oh, yes, that *other* Jack. Going home wasn't going to be peaceful any more. Maybe she could ignore him. You weren't supposed to have to give counseling to your neighbors. Yes, she was a repository for the broken, but not on her own time. He could go pound sand.

* * * *

The only things he had pounded in were some fence posts. She saw them in a neatly ordered row, meticulously spaced where the stone walls had been. The mound on Jack's grave was all that was left and the lunatic was running a Bobcat into the woods, dumping the rest. A tractor with post-hole digger attached sat on the grass. Slinging her purse over her shoulder, Marjorie walked across their mutual-but-becoming-his yard, planting herself where he would have to run over her.

Apparently, he wasn't quite willing. After making an intimidating run, he stopped the Bobcat inches from her feet, throttling back. It was still a loud little thing, belching smoke.

"What are you doing?" she yelled.

"I told you, I don't like walls." He was pretty deeply tanned despite his blond hair, indicating that he spent some time outside, probably demolishing things. Didn't he work? Or sleep? He'd been at it since before she left for work and she left early.

"What are you going to have in here?" She was still yelling and he turned the Bobcat off, straining to hear her.

"Horses."

"Horses?!"

"Why?" he asked, a little ominously. "Don't you like horses?"

"I love them." She pointed in the direction of the back of her property. "I have a barn, in case you haven't noticed." It was where she had hoped to have a pony someday, if she had children, though the chances of that were looking slim. Her biological clock had started winding down as Jeff stepped out on her. Just when they had the house and the picket fence, he made sure she didn't get the rest. She wondered now if that timing was strictly accidental or whether her plans for a family had freaked him out. He had never seemed totally on board with that. Maybe she shouldn't have ignored the warning signals.

"You call that thing a barn?"

It was a three-stall shed row. Terming it a barn was generous. Still, she didn't like to be insulted.

"Well, you don't even have one!"

"Not yet."

"Yet?" she echoed. "Do you have a permit?"

"What do you think?"

"I don't think you'd bother," she retorted.

He wiped his forehead, dripping sweat again. "You're on my property."

"Well, you were on mine."

"Yes, but I was helping you."

"I'm helping you. I'm telling you that you need a permit."

"Oh, thank you." His tone was acid. If she'd been a stone, it would have etched her. "Look, Miss Intellectual, I know what I need a permit for and there are going to be horses. You're living in the country now."

"Miss Intellectual?"

"Yeah, look at you. Matching purse and shoes, your underwear probably matches too. Nice preppy clothes. Or do they call them yuppie now?"

"My underwear is none of your concern."

"It is when it's hanging through your shorts."

"What IS your problem?" she demanded. "I don't even know you."

"Good," he said, and cranked up the machine again. Gunning it, he wove his way around her, proceeding on his demented way.

That guy got burned, she thought. *She probably wore matching underwear.*

She still hadn't eaten the hamburger she had threatened him with the previous night. Putting on a pot of water to boil for corn on the cob, she lugged her grill onto the front porch and then down onto the flagstone walk, near but not too near the hammock strung between two trees. She didn't want to flambee herself, though God knew it was hot enough. Pouring in charcoal, she fired the brickettes in several places and went back inside to pour a gin and tonic. A cold drink and a lie-down in the hammock were in order.

Unfortunately, her rest was disrupted by the grind of the little Bobcat, heroically attempting to do more than it was designed to do. He was going to burn that sucker up, she thought vindictively, and then let him tell her she knew nothing about the country. She could run one of those machines herself. She had done it, dumping gravel in the mud pit in front of her shed row.

That guy had no idea.

He annoyed her so badly she had a second drink, then gave up and went inside where she couldn't hear the noise over the hum of the air conditioner. A year and a half of a nice quiet neighbor, and now she had Mad Max. If tomorrow wasn't too hectic, she should probably drop by the township building and sniff around. The women there had seemed cordial despite her yuppie roots when she had hacked down snow-covered branches on the road with a chain saw, saving the road crew the trouble. It had earned her brownie points. Maybe it was time to cash them in.

* * * *

"Jack Calloway?"

Joan, the secretary at their small municipality, sounded surprised. A tiny little Irish lady, she had been in her job for thirty-five years and knew every inch of her rural domain and everyone in it.

"He's in compliance," she said. "Do you have an issue?"

"No real issue," Marjorie said, deflated. "I just thought I'd check. He's been so unpleasant, I wondered if he was putting up something illegal."

"No." Joan's tone was carefully neutral, her official 'I'm not getting into this' voice. "That property is zoned residential/agricultural, the same as yours, so he can have as many horses as his pasture allows. Which, if I'm not mistaken, is a good many. Mrs. Clements had a number of acres."

"Sixteen," Marjorie said promptly.

"Well, it's two acres for the first horse and an additional acre for each additional horse, so I'm sure you can do the math. And technically he's farming. Horses are agriculture. That means he can run equipment at any time needed, especially if he's baling hay."

Alerted by her training to nuances in conversation, Marjorie sensed that she was losing ground. Who was this guy, anyway? If he was related to someone prominent or an old family or even just someone well-liked, she wasn't going to get very far.

"Is he anybody I should know about?"

"Not especially," Joan said. "He's an adjunct professor over at Presser's." It was the local community college.

"Professor? That's interesting."

And he had called her Miss Intellectual.

"They're off for the summer. I'm sure things will get quieter come fall."

"Oh, that's good." Deliberately vague now, Marjorie passed a little more time in innocuous remarks, then made her departure, home to the rattle, bang and clank of the Bobcat.

Chapter Three

It was a long, loud week, but forewarned by her conversation with Joan, Marjorie kept carefully away from her neighbor. Saturday was a beef and beer at the firehouse, a fundraiser, and she had determined to go because they also had an animal rescue bringing pets. She hadn't entirely given up on the thought of getting a dog. Sandy Kennedy, whose husband had walked out and left her flat, ran an unofficial doggie day care at her home hidden on top of a hill accessible only by a torturous stone driveway. Technically, it was illegal—against the zoning—but everyone knew she was hanging on by the skin of her teeth and looked the other way as she tried to keep her home. Marjorie could look the other way, too.

The day dawned clear, less hot and humid, so after tormenting her hair for a while, she put on some not obscenely short shorts, sandals and peasant blouse and jumped in her Subaru wagon for the short trip to the fire company. Staffed by volunteers, it was next to the horse show grounds that also hosted dog shows, a country fair and a blues concert. Whenever triangular pieces of red, white and blue plastic fluttered from the posts of the fire company sign, you knew there was an event. She knew people now and a friendly crowd had gathered, including the organizer of the animal rescue with her volunteers. Marjorie noted their location before getting her food, because in case she left with a pup she wanted to get fed first. That was how the fire company made their money. For four bucks and a wait at a food truck manned by volunteers, she got a hot roast beef sandwich dripping gravy onto a roll the size of a submarine, plus a forkful of coleslaw and a generous plastic cup of beer. Much of the food was donated, so it was a deal.

"Hey, Helen," she greeted the head of the rescue, whom she knew, once she had eaten. A tall, earthy farm girl who had spent her life around animals, Helen had a passion for rescuing them. "Got any goats?"

For a moment, Helen seemed to take her seriously. "Goats?"

Marjorie shook her head, laughing, "No, I'm kidding you. But I am thinking about a puppy. Jack the Cat shuffled off his mortal coil."

"Oh, no! What happened?"

"No clue, unless it was heat stroke. He had plenty of shade, plus he could come in the basement window to where it was cool, so I don't know. I found him on the roof. Not a mark on him. He was just at the vet for shots. They said he was fine. I have no idea. Really shook me up, though."

"I guess. I'm sorry. Well, we have pups. Looking for anything special?"

"I have coyotes out back in the woods, so it can't be small. Pit, maybe?"

"Yeah, they have a better chance. You intend to keep it in the yard, right? 'Yotes will climb fences sometimes, though, so you'll still have to be careful."

"I know," Marjorie said. "I've got a .22. I just got a new neighbor, too, and he's running equipment back and forth, putting up a barn. I won't let the dog run."

"Good. Come look," Helen invited.

There were a couple of tabby cats that pulled at her heartstrings, but Marjorie thought this time she wanted a dog. She needed a dog. A year and a half alone was beginning to wear on her and although she knew they were work, she preferred a puppy she could raise her own way.

Helen hadn't exaggerated. She had a whole gaggle of puppies, some of which looked like Yorkies—too small. But every rescue had pitties and this one was no different. In a wire pen, a group of roly poly pit pups that looked related were busy chewing on each other, tails wagging in the air like little stove pipes.

"Oh, my God," Marjorie said, kneeling down. "How do you pick?"

"You let them pick you," Helen suggested.

The first one to her was a gray and white spotted male with blue eyes and floppy ears. The others came screeching over, of course, leaping on the wire and chewing her fingers, but the male simply leaned through, head on her thigh, gazing up at her with smoky eyes as if she was manna from Heaven.

"Oh, my God," Marjorie said again, hearing Helen starting to laugh above her.

"Told you."

"Oh, yes." Marjorie stood, leaning over the wire to pick up the squirming puppy, dodging a stream of pee as he let loose. "You gonna pee all over my house?" she asked, snuggling him. "Yes, you are. I know, I know. Well, it's OK. We aren't fancy."

"You going to get day care for him?" Helen asked. "I know you work long hours."

"Sandy Kennedy said she'll take him as long as he's had his shots."

"Everything," Helen confirmed. "Completely up to date. He'll need to be neutered in a few more months, but as long as you bring me proof of the surgery, I'll refund you $65."

"Good deal," Marjorie agreed. "How much are you getting for your pups now?"

"Three hundred," Helen told her. "I know you're a good home, so I'll throw in food and a bed. Do you have a crate?"

"One to start," Marjorie confirmed, "although I'll get him something bigger. You know he'll end up in bed with me, though."

"Beach towel," Helen advised. "Put him on that on a pillow

next to your head so you can feel him squirming when he needs to go out. And don't plan on getting much sleep."

"I don't, anyway," Marjorie said, rooting for her credit card. "The new neighbor is running equipment day and night."

"Place next to you?" Helen nodded. "I heard. Shame about Mrs. Clements, but she did have a good, long life."

"Yeah, well, I'd like to give the guy who bought the place a short one."

"Jack Calloway? What's wrong with him?"

Did everybody else know this guy? "Oh, nothing, I guess," Marjorie backtracked. "He's just noisy, putting up a barn, and I'm used to it being quiet. I'll adjust."

Helen shrugged. "Jack can be a little prickly sometimes, but he's OK."

"I noticed," Marjorie said, snuggling the pup. "He buried Jack for me, though. I didn't ask. He just came over and did it."

"Yeah, he would. He always helps the fire company, too, any time they need something." Helen looked at her with a hint of laughter in her eyes. "If he finally settled on a place, try to live with it. He won't be going anywhere. He's stubborn as a mule."

"Great," Marjorie muttered.

"He was set to marry Griffy's daughter," Helen passed along an interesting tidbit. John Griffin was a crusty old dairy farmer, well known in the community. His cows routinely took themselves from pasture to barn and back again, promptly twice a day, blocking traffic at regular hours. You just tried to avoid that road at milking time. Marjorie recalled hearing he had a daughter who was a little wild.

"That the girl that was sniffing gas at the vet's?" she inquired.

"Same one." Helen shrugged. "One of them backed out, probably him. But it sounds like he's putting down roots anyway."

"Yeah, right next to me," Marjorie groused.

This time Helen did laugh. "Get ready for a barn raising."

"What?" Their community had taken some time for Marjorie to understand but, she had incorporated it. Rural WASP for the most part, some German and Scotch-Irish stock with an infusion of Pennsylvania Dutch from over the county border. You could roll a bowling ball through the place without hitting a person of any color. "He's Dutch?"

"No," Helen said, "but they like him. They'll do a barn raising for him."

"More fun and frolic," Marjorie moaned. "At least they'll get it over quickly."

"Day or two," Helen agreed. "Better for you."

"I hope."

"Well, he likes dogs," Helen pointed out. "He got a border collie from me years ago. I don't think he has him any more, but he should like your pittie. Got a name for him?"

She had a name for Jack, Marjorie thought, but not one she would disclose. She looked down at the puppy, using her knuckle like a bone. "Maybe Blue. I love his little blue eyes."

"I think he'll be a porker later on," Helen observed. "Look at his feet. But that's not a bad thing for you, all alone out there like you are. Come on, let's get him some food."

They were hoisting a bag of puppy chow into the deck of the Subaru, parked in the dusty field near the horse show ring, when there was a sound of a truck backfiring and a crew of men drove in past them. Bemused, Helen and Marjorie watched as Jack the Jerk himself descended from the truck with a group of volunteer firemen. He was entrenched, apparently. She was only surprised she hadn't seen him before, but perhaps she had, not noticing him then because he wasn't annoying her. His hair looked a little less Neanderthal than it had, as if he'd finally taken time out from his labors to get spiffed up. He was good-looking, she had to admit, lean and yet muscular in the requisite tight-fitting Levis and a plaid shirt. Not Madras—that would have marked him as a dreaded yuppie that moved out from the city and then tried to remake the country into the city they had left. Marjorie had been accepted because she never tried to do that. Plus, he had a great butt.

He nodded to them, rendered a little more communicative

by the presence of friends.

"Gettin' a pup?"

Marjorie just nodded.

"Good idea."

"You want one?" Helen put in. "I hear you have a place now."

He gave Marjorie a quick glance, discerning at once that she had been discussing him.

"Maybe later. Pretty busy right now."

"Well, you know where to find me," Helen laughed. "Cleaning poop out of kennels."

She hadn't thought he had it in him, but Jack smiled. "I'll look you up. Gotta go buy a hat before I end up like Marjorie's cat."

"You think it was the heat, then?" Still anxious for an answer, wondering what she could have done wrong, Marjorie would stoop to questioning the only other witness.

"Most likely," her nemesis said. "Black cat like that, went to sleep on the roof, never woke up. Sun's strong up there. Probably felt good and then he slept away. You'd think he'd have the sense to come down, but they don't always."

Like the frog in the boiling water thing, Marjorie thought. Didn't notice the heat till it cooked him. She had to hope it was that, anyway. She didn't want to think he'd been hit on the road and dragged himself home to die. But Jack wasn't a cat you could keep in.

Probably the other Jack was the same way, too.

Chapter Four

After the first night of carrying a peeing puppy down the steps every two hours, Marjorie slept in her recliner in the living room with Blue in her lap. Cuddled on a thick beach towel, nose stuffed in her crotch, he was the perfect puppy. It was something of a jolt to drop him off at Sandy's every morning promptly at 7:30, and expensive, but on the other hand she knew he was getting the best possible care and a little bit of training. He was going to be a big, powerful dog one day and having manners would be important. Sandy's herd of dogs and cats would socialize him if anything would, and she had visitors of all stripes. He was already a friendly pup.

It was a good thing. On Friday evening, Marjorie returned home to the sight of what looked like a small fleet of trucks next door. Some were pickups, but a lot were work trucks stacked with loads of tied-down lumber, spaced out around the site of the proposed barn. Tellingly, she noted a yellow-orange building permit in a plastic sleeve staked to a wooden signpost, glaringly obvious in Jack's front yard. It was a message to anyone who cared to look, but it was meant for her and she knew it.

Chaos began at sunrise. Roused by the sound of both engines and horse shoes, she rolled over with a groan, accidentally propelling Blue out of his comfy nest and onto the hardwood floor, where he promptly squatted and peed.

"Sorry, my fault," she apologized, watching as urine hit the boards and the puppy looked up in perfect innocence, squinting his little blue eyes in his wrinkled face.

It was too late for the floor, but she called him to the back door, lifting him down the steps and out into the yard. On Jack's side, she could see a rapidly growing army of English, Amish and Mennonites. The Dutch called everyone who was not Dutch "English," but in this case it was apt. Naively, she had taken Jack for an Irishman, but when she ran his surname through a genealogy search, curious about the name, it was English--descended from Norman conquerors and named for some village in France she couldn't pronounce. Well, he had called her Miss Intellectual. She might as well live up to it.

In any case, it was infrequent that the two groups mixed, so she supposed he must have magic working for him. She recognized some of his good-old-boy friends, but there were more Dutchmen in black pants, white shirts and straw hats they would need because it promised to be another scorcher. There were buggies lined up in a row, shafts resting on the ground, and horses and mules in harness tied in a circular group, swatting flies off each other. Apparently, some of the Dutch didn't mind electricity or perhaps Jack's friends were sawing, but she heard the whine of power tools and smelled sawdust.

Blue was pacing the fence line, doing his best guard dog job with ferocious puppy barks and growls.

"Blue, c'mon," she called him for breakfast. It was already hot and she didn't want another Jack the Cat incident. They would both be better off inside.

That was what she told herself, anyway. Eventually, she couldn't stand not knowing what was going on. The Dutch would be scandalized by the sight of a woman's legs, so out of respect for their customs she put on a long, loose cotton skirt and a top without cleavage. She didn't have much of that, anyway. Then she walked out on the road with Blue in her arms because the macadam was too hot for his paws, peering curiously at the work.

It looked like an ant hill, with a framework already up and men hammering on rafters, lifting beams by ropes. The women had arrived, carrying innumerable casseroles into the back kitchen. They would feed the men promptly at noon, then they would work like demons until milking time. Depending on the size of the intended barn, which didn't seem as large as she had feared, they might finish in one day. No one worked on Sunday, of course, so they had every incentive to finish. That suited Marjorie.

Eventually the women spotted the puppy and came to the edge of the road, intercepting her very politely. They looked like flowers in their multi-colored gowns and stringed bonnets, accompanied in some cases by reticent, adorable children, the boys with typical soup-bowl haircuts and the little girls braided. They hung by their mothers, not approaching a stranger until given permission.

"Can we see him?" one woman asked, and Marjorie stopped, obligingly.

"How cute!" another put in as they crowded around, offering hands for Blue to lick. "It is a pit bull?"

"Yes." Marjorie knew many of the Dutch raised puppies for sale—not very kindly, in a lot of cases—yet in their way, they were fond of animals. They simply saw them as merchandise and raised those most likely to sell quickly—popular breeds, not pits.

"He will be nice?" one woman asked, sounding dubious. But she was petting him.

"If he is raised well," Marjorie assured her. "They are like their owners, usually. If you're nice, they're nice."

The smiling woman cornered her eyes at Marjorie. "Then you must be nice. He is very sweet."

She laughed, thinking this woman must not have talked to Jack. "I try."

Apparently encouraged, the same woman persisted. "There is not much in this kitchen. Do you think we might warm a couple of things in your oven?"

"Oh, yes, of course." Why not, she thought. The Dutch

women were fabulous cooks. She wracked her brains to remember if the oven was clean. It was. They were meticulous housekeepers, too. She didn't have time to be one of those, but hopefully the house would pass muster. If not, they would be too polite to say so.

"My back door is open," she said. "Come in through the gate and the fenced yard and there is a back kitchen. Go through to the oven."

"Thank you," they said in a chorus.

"I have a shed row, with fans, too," she offered, feeling sorry for their horses. "If you have some suffering badly from the heat, you can put them in. There is a water pump, just bring buckets."

In for a penny, in for a pound.

They sounded like a flock of doves, thanking her in sometimes accented English. The children were enthralled by the puppy and eventually she put him down on the grass where, encircled by children, he could roll and amuse them. Finally, they began to laugh, petting his chubby belly as their mothers chattered, and they were just a group of women, recognizable in any culture.

As if alerted by instinct, Marjorie looked up to see their host coming across the yard, blond hair beneath a tractor hat, clad in denim, his shirt sleeveless due to the heat. That shirt outlined a really good body and his arms were muscular, tanned and sporting soft golden hair on his forearms. He was attractive, she thought reluctantly. Too bad he was such a grouch. She wondered what Jenny Griffin had done to put him off.

But apparently today he had decided to be on his best behavior. "How's the pup?"

"Great."

"I wouldn't bring him over here," he said. "He'll get squished. But if you want to crate him and come for dinner, come over."

Dinner was lunch and everybody knew when it was. Twelve o'clock. People ate at six, twelve and six, without exception. If she was loaning out her oven and her shed, Marjorie decided, she would accept.

"OK," she said. These were nice people—friendly, respectful. Not the catty Beverly Hills wanna-bees she had left behind.

It felt like this was where she belonged.

Women buzzed in and out of her kitchen, three horses were in the shed with hay and water, and eventually it was time to eat. The smell of everything cooking had made Marjorie ravenous, so she kissed Blue, removed his collar to prevent any strangling, and put him in his crate with a peanut-butter-stuffed Kong and the AC running. Although he whined when she left and she knew there would be a brief period of barking, he would settle. And she was starving.

Some of the other neighbors had drifted in—people who had been walking their dogs or pushing strollers and stayed, invited by the others. She even saw the Zoning Officer, the guy who would have to issue Jack's final permit, and smiled. He did know his way around. People were bringing out blankets, buckets, benches, lawn chairs, anything to sit on, while the women utilized truck beds to roll out the food. There was everything: the beef jerky they called boys' legs in gravy, sausage, brown butter noodles that made her stomach clench, potato filling, cabbage rolls, ham loaf, tuna salad, potato salad, macaroni salad, pepper hash. She saw apple salad, corn pudding and something that looked like a lot of peaches and cream dotted with marshmallows. Cheese, pickles, pickled okra, pickled beets, deviled eggs. Chow-chow. Apple butter. Bread. Butter so fresh that it was never salted because it didn't need preserving. And that didn't even count dessert, plus one entire truck bed full of lemonade, birch beer, iced tea and ice. There would be no booze here. She couldn't imagine where to start, but before she could get into it there was a hush and a bearded older man stood up, bowing his head. He wore black pants with suspenders, a dark plaid shirt in defiance of custom and a hat, but she knew he had to be an Elder.

He got right to the point. "We thank Thee, Oh Heavenly Father, for this food we are about to eat. Amen."

There was a chorus of "Amens" and then a discreet rush for

the food.

She had brought her own lawn chair, so once she had filled her plate and taken lemonade, Marjorie sat under one of the shade trees in what had been Mrs. Clements's back yard.

"What are you thinking?" That voice was becoming a little bit familiar, as was the directness of the question. She glanced up at Jack with a faint smile. He was standing with a plate in his hand, following her gaze toward the back-kitchen door.

"About Mrs. Clements," she answered honestly. "I was just thinking she would be shocked at what you've done with the place, but not upset. She was raised on a farm, she loved animals, so this would probably make her happy."

"I never knew her," he responded. "Just dealt with the family. They wanted a buyer who wouldn't put up a bunch of houses, so it worked."

Marjorie sighed. "I didn't want somebody who would put up a bunch of houses, either. So at least thanks for that. And for burying Jack."

He blinked. "Your cat was named Jack?"

She started to laugh. "I swear. Yes. He really was. Jack the Cat."

That finally got a smile out of him. He had a good smile, faintly sardonic, but definitely amused. Apparently, he could laugh at himself. She had taken him as way too uptight for that.

"How many horses do you want here?" she changed the subject.

"Oh, half a dozen. Not big. I'd like one for myself and then it's always a good idea to take boarders. Lot of work, but it pays for yours and a little extra. Do you ride?"

"Not in years," Marjorie said. "Pony rides."

"But you bought a place with a barn," he pointed out.

"Shed row," she corrected. "I was thinking maybe a pony or two, when I can afford them. Rescues, maybe. Just give them a safe home. You know—something nobody else wants."

He gave her a speculative look. "What's your job?"

"I'm a social worker at Hopemont. You know the place?"

"Sure. I teach at Presser's. We've had a few of your graduates there."

"Well, some of them do get out alive," she said. "Teach what?"

"History."

Marjorie could feel her eyebrows elevate, involuntarily. "History. And you called me Miss Intellectual?"

She thought he had the grace to look slightly abashed. "That was more a matter of appearance," he finally said. "You look like you just stepped out of suburbia. Very buttoned-down. I equate that with snottiness, sometimes."

"Well, I can be snotty," she admitted. "You scared me to

death, that's all. I had no idea this house had been sold or there was anybody over here. And you didn't seem exactly thrilled with the sight of me, either."

"Ah, you were coming apart," he said. "I didn't want a meltdown."

Yes, she thought, anger had kept her going through that. At least now they were having a civilized conversation.

"Don't judge a book by its cover," she responded. "I did step out of suburbia, because I wanted to step out. I like it here. And I've still got my yuppie wardrobe because it's what I've got. Good clothes are expensive. It costs to fix up an old house."

"Yeah, I know. This place is costing me a fortune."

Adjunct professors didn't make much, she knew. Like social work, that was something you did because you felt called to it. Nobody paid well for a calling. Jack was probably in hock up to his eyeballs. It accounted for why he was doing so much of the work himself, and of course there would be no charge for the barn raising. For the people who did it, that was a calling, too.

Chapter Five

Monday, 6 a.m., the trucks rolled in. Marjorie turned in her recliner, awakened by Blue's growls as his ears swiveled.

"Ugh," she said. Jack had a barn, but no fence, just posts. This would be the fencing crew.

Blue was beginning to negotiate steps, so she put him down to go out for the requisite pee, shadowing him. Still alert to coyotes and hawks, she carried her .22.

Men in hats and overalls were stringing strong tensile wire run through white poly cable. Animals could see the color and the stuff was strong as heck, so they seldom ran through it or got tangled. She could hear the click of staple guns and the hum of conversation, but duty called, so she couldn't wait to see how it turned out. There would be a little horse paradise by the time she got back. The barn was already princely—solid board with a loft, six stalls and a tack room, and a metal roof painted with stuff that reflected heat so the horses didn't cook. Unlike the Dutch, Jack would have electricity so he could run fans and she had seen the system of sprayers overhead in each stall. A fine mist of bug spray would help the fly problem.

She dressed quickly, a light cotton dress for the heat, loaded up her puppy and left.

"Who've we got this morning?" she asked Karen. This time she had prepared, stopping off at the small convenience store on the outskirts of the park she drove through on the way to work so she could pick up coffee

"Tommy," the receptionist told her and she smiled, making a mental note to watch her arms. She wore a sleeveless dress and Tommy, a very impaired non-verbal child, had a way of expressing his affection by biting the top of her shoulder when she wasn't watching him. It was like Blue nipping for attention, but a lot more hazardous. Although she'd had her hepatitis shot, she wasn't going to have time for the nurse to patch her up again.

Fortunately, his parents were with him. Tommy had reached the limits of what they could do for him and his family was going to try putting him in day school. This was not a family that had put their obligation on others--they wanted him back. It was not Marjorie's decision, of course. The clinical team working with Tommy had decided he was ready to go and she was simply the paper pusher.

After that it was another evaluation, a teenager who had terrorized his neighborhood by dressing in camo and lurking outside their windows at night. Nobody had ever been able to prove that he was armed. If he was, he'd been very careful about hiding his weapon, but after an hour with the clinical team, Marjorie felt pretty sure he had one and would use it someday. The others concurred and she returned to her office to call the referral source in an effort to dissuade them from their position that he was just a troubled boy from a poor family situation. His family situation was poor because his parents were afraid he was going to kill them. An open residential treatment center was not where you put a kid like that. He needed juvenile detention.

Lunch finally happened about three o'clock, a tuna sandwich Karen had brought her from the lunchroom and kept in their tiny fridge. Marjorie wolfed it down, pinching the waistband of her dress to confirm her notion that she was losing weight. She was slim and slight of build and all those skipped lunches didn't help. Maybe Jack was right and she was getting scrawny.

Now why was she thinking about that sourpuss in the middle of the afternoon? She knew why. Her hormones were stirring. There had been no one since Jeff. But, she thought, given a little incentive, she might jump Jack Calloway's bones and she didn't think he'd fight it. He hadn't stopped to talk to her every time he saw her for nothing. It was purely physical, of course. She didn't even like him. But he was cute.

Don't go there, Marjorie, she told herself. *He has issues with women. You're a professional. You know what's going on in his head.*

But it wasn't his brain she was thinking about.

* * * *

She was right, horse paradise was nearly at her doorstep when she got back, just without horses. She supposed those would come soon enough—a caravan of trucks, horse vans and manure on the road while Jack filled up his little kingdom.

Blue skidded on the hardwood floors through the cabin, making a beeline for the back door and his pee place. Though Sandy assured her that he sprinkled her place liberally, he had to go at once to his spot in the yard, as if assuring the world he was back. Marjorie followed, .22 cradled in her arms. Nothing was going to eat her pup.

Jack was inspecting his fence line. Alerted by Blue's furious barks, he glanced up in time to see her carrying armament.

"Hey," he said, strolling over to the fence. "It isn't that bad, is it?"

Marjorie smiled. "Coyotes and hawks. He's still pretty small."

Jack pushed back his tractor hat. "He looks like he'll go about eighty pounds, so later you won't have to worry. But, yeah, they'll snatch him now." He gestured to her rifle. "You know how to use that thing?"

"I know how to use this thing."

"Just checking," he said. "Those bullets carry a distance."

"I won't hit you. Not unless I mean to."

He grinned. "Well, I've been warned. Um, I've got an

entire freezer full of food from Saturday. Take anything you want; I'll never eat it all."

The thought of not cooking was highly appealing, as was the thought of a repeat. "OK. Let me feed the brat and I'll come over."

"You can bring him," Jack said.

He had not torn down the handicapped ramp Mrs. Clements had used for her husband, so Marjorie let Blue run up the ramp to Jack's door where he immediately stood up, trying to peer inside. She preferred knocking.

It was the requisite dinner hour, the crew was gone and he was in, probably eating leftovers. He answered her knock promptly, opening the door and letting the puppy inside.

"He'll pee," she warned him.

"Most pups do. I'm going to shred this carpet anyway."

Mrs. Clements had kept the house just as it was the day her husband died, like some sort of shrine. There was a lot that needed shredding. Marjorie stepped in with a certain sense of trepidation.

Following Jack into the kitchen, she saw that her feeling was justified. Everything he had done was outside. The inside was a jumble of curtainless windows, stacked cartons and furniture still under plastic moving wrap. It had all the cheer of a cave. The only thing that appeared to work was a new television, set to the weather channel.

"This is going to take some work," she said, shooing Blue off one of the cartons. He still did the puppy squat, but it was inevitable that he would start lifting his leg and there was a lot of stuff in squirting range.

"Outside first, while the weather's still good," Jack said. "I can deal with this when it's snowing."

"What're you going to do with it?" She was still following him to the back kitchen, where Mrs. Clements had had a freezer. She was betting it was still there.

"Paint the paneling." Marjorie nodded. It was the 60s style dark paneling everybody had used, increasing the house's resemblance to a cave. "Refinish the floors. They're not bad, under that carpet. New cabinets. The stuff in the kitchen is all from the 50s. I found an Elvis lamp in the basement entry."

Marjorie giggled. "Yeah, they were here, I guess, about sixty years."

Jack grunted softly, going through the doorway to the back kitchen where the old freezer still hummed away. "Help yourself, I swear there's enough in here to feed an army. I'll bring you a carton if you want."

"Holy moley." Marjorie peered inside. "You weren't kidding."

Sixty years, she thought silently, loading up. Neither had more than a high school education, but they had worked like troupers, paying everything but their mortgage in cash. Mr. Clements had worked six days a week in a steel mill, getting two holidays per year—July 4th and Christmas. When they went on strike, he and his wife delivered newspapers at 4 a.m. They had raised most of their own food. He only went to a doctor when he was dying because doctors cost money, even though Medicare would have paid for it. They had thought they were living the American Dream because they had a house.

"Such good people," she said. "I used to come over on holidays and watch old Westerns with Mrs. Clements. We both enjoyed it. She never got cable, of course. Too expensive and she didn't understand how it worked."

"A dying breed," Jack said.

"You from here?" she asked. "You seem to know everybody."

"Sellersville." It was near the county line, sharing a consolidated school district with theirs. "We all went to school together, so yeah, I know people. I always lived there, then I moved here. It's closer to work."

It had been closer to Jenny Griffin, too, but she wouldn't mention that.

"Still got family?" she wondered.

"Some."

It didn't sound like he wanted to explore that subject, so

neither did she.

"You?" he asked.

Marjorie laughed. "Yuppieville. Over near Hopemont. My husband and I had a McMansion. He wasn't up for much more than that, though. Ended up losing it anyway, in the divorce settlement. There was no way I could afford to live there, so I found the cabin. Commuting is cheaper."

"Makes sense," Jack admitted, "if you can adapt. The power failures didn't scare you off, huh?"

Marjorie laughed. What everybody called their rural-f'd-up-electric was like a Third World nation.

"Well, I keep a lot of bottled water," she admitted. "And a woodstove. Generator would be nice, but that's a lot of money."

"I know electricians," Jack offered. "If you ever do think you can swing it, I'll see if I can get you a deal. You really don't want to live out here without one."

"I know," she groaned, closing the door on the freezer. "That's all I have room for."

"You have a back kitchen," Jack pointed out. "Get a little RV refrigerator. Works off bottled gas. You've got extra storage, plus food when the power goes out."

"Really?"

"Yeah, it can save you plenty. Here." He held out his hands for the carton. "I'll carry it over for you."

Marjorie was a little startled by the thought, but not unwilling. She'd let him as far as the front door. "I'll get the pup."

He didn't ask to come in, didn't do anything but hand her the carton when they got there. She could get it to the kitchen or even unload in parts if she needed to. Much as she might entertain some fantasies about Jack, she didn't want him in her house. Not yet.

Chapter Six

Marjorie's fear of Paradise Lost seemed to have been overrated.

There were a couple of horse vans that came in on weekends, accompanied by people who parked considerately on the other side of Jack's barn where she didn't see them. She knew the horses were there only by their appearance in the pasture and they weren't what she had expected, either.

"Look, Blue," she said, hunkered down inside her fence, peering through. Her now twenty-five pound pup, fattening up for winter, licked her fingers instead of following the direction they were pointing. He apparently didn't care about the horses.

There were two, gleaming animals with the fine lines of Thoroughbred breeding, but one was in leg wraps and limped, while the other bore visible scars.

"Bowed tendon and a trailer accident," Jack's voice came from behind one of the humongous bushes left by Mrs. Clements. She wasn't sure whether he took a subtle pleasure in scaring her or there were just too many obstacles in that yard. He was pruning, so probably it was the latter. That particular bush reminded her of an ostrich, just bigger. Much bigger.

"Bowed what?" A trailer accident she understood, but the

rest was Greek.

"Bowed tendon. Got raced too hard, too soon, and the tendon in his foreleg shredded."

"Good God, will it heal?"

"Not totally. With care, it'll build scar tissue. He'll always have a thick-looking leg. Can't race again, of course."

"Then what do you do with him?" Discovered now, she stood up, looking at him and wondering why Blue hadn't told her he was there. Then she realized it was because the dog was so used to him. He regarded him as a member of his pack. Any time he got loose, he ran straight to Jack's front door. The damn dog loved him.

"Well, usually he'd end up in Blue's dish," Jack said. "But his owners think a lot of him, so they sent him here to rehab. Could end up staying, I suppose. They have the money."

"Must be nice," she said. "You rehab horses? I thought you worked." She had seen his truck pulling out in the mornings, returning in the late afternoon.

"No reason I can't do both. Mostly you just feed them and medicate them twice a day. Nature does the rest. Good grass, plenty of water, no stress. And as much as these owners are paying for lay-up board, I don't have to take in any more, at least right now. Nice quiet life for everybody."

"Great," she said.

"You want to help?"

"Me?" she squeaked. "I don't know anything about horses."

"Easy peasy," he said. "You run water out of a hose over the gray horse's leg. He loves it, never moves. Want to try?"

"Can Blue come?" She hated for the dog to see her from the yard, unable to reach her.

"Sure, if you watch him. If he gets kicked, though, you're going to have a vet bill."

She looked at her dog, torn. But if Jack was there, that dog wasn't going anywhere. He wouldn't leave him if a team of buffalo went down the road. She almost wished he would get a dog of his own and stop stealing hers.

"OK," she decided, not questioning why she had so much faith in Jack's abilities. They weren't close, exactly, they might just speak a couple times a week.

The gray horse had a long racing name, but Jack just called him Oliver. He was a friendly soul, offering his nose to be petted and nuzzling Blue, who was startled but soon settled down under a tree, chewing a stick. Marjorie had realized that her dog essentially had no nerves. He was the ultimate lazy pit bull.

"Here," Jack coaxed. "I put this lead shank over his nose, like so." She watched as he ran the chain portion of the shank through the ring of the horse's halter and across his nose, hooking it to the ring on the other side. "That just gives you a little extra control to keep him from moving around too much while you're hosing him. Never yank on it. It hurts. It's just...having brakes."

He handed her the hose, already running cold water.

"From the knee to the hoof," Jack said. "Like so." He put his hand over hers, directing the spray, and she felt the contact all the way to her bones. No one had touched her in a long, long time. She felt something sweet and fateful move through her. Jack was hitting on her—very subtly—and she didn't mind.

"Why are his feet black and white?" she asked. "Are they supposed to be?

"Not usually," Jack said, "but he's a light color. He's gray, so the pigment in his hooves is different. Some people think they're weak feet, but I've seen plenty that can run."

He released her hand, running his fingers gently down the back of the horse's foreleg. "This just wasn't one of them. He'll never run again."

"Poor boy," Marjorie said, stroking the horse's forelock. He rubbed on her hand, but as soon as she stopped, his head went down and he started ripping at the grass.

"That's OK," Jack said. "Let him eat. That way he doesn't notice the water. It'll help the inflammation. Don't let him step on the shank, though. You don't want to yank his nose. They don't trust you if you let them get hurt."

"In that case," she said tartly, "he shouldn't trust anybody. They let him get hurt."

"That's the way of the world, Marjorie," Jack said quietly. "We all get hurt. You just have to know who you can trust."

It wasn't a conversation she wanted to have. "How do you know about horses?"

"I worked when I was a kid up at the Fairlawn Racetrack. You know it?"

Marjorie nodded.

"I needed extra money and I liked horses, so I used to work up there once I was able to get my hands on a car. I was sixteen. Interesting place. I learned a lot, mostly that I didn't want to do it for a living."

"Hard work, low pay?" she guessed.

"Yep, tough life. My father always told me to work smart, not hard, I'd come out better that way. He was right. Teaching isn't great money-wise, but it beats being a hot walker."

"A what?"

"Less than a groom," he explained. "And it doesn't pay squat."

"Whew," she said, watching Oliver mow down the grass. "But it does make you some money this way?"

"That's why I built the barn."

"I can see you doing this," Marjorie conceded. "But

history? Really?"

He just smiled very slightly. "How are you going to know where you're going if you don't know where you've been? Remember fractals?"

She did. One semester of geometry had taught her the sequence that lent itself to every design in nature, depending upon where you set the points that sculpted the design. Everything from the paisley in a dress to a flower petal or the shape of a porpoise—you could create every design, like the work of God, over and over in every facet of creation. She had regarded it as no less than sublime, speaking of a higher order.

"I tell my students history is just a fractal, repeating over and over in a pattern you can discern if you know what the set points are. And if you know that, you can change the pattern. Or not. For the most part, we don't. That's why we keep making the same stupid mistakes, over and over."

"Profound," she said. Jack had abandoned the tractor hat with the advent of cooler weather and, for the first time, she dared something. She'd been wanting to do it, but questioned whether it was wise. Now, understanding that this man was much, much more than she had thought, she didn't care. Very gently, with her free hand, she stroked back a stand of his corn-silk hair, tapping gently on his forehead.

"Good brain in there, Professor."

He froze, for just an instant, and she wondered if she had made that mistake she feared. But then he smiled.

"Thank you, Doctor."

"Not quite a doctor," she corrected. "I only got my Masters."

He drew back very slightly, but it was to twist the handle on the water pump, cutting off Oliver's flow. "That's it. When his leg dries, I'll bandage him up again. Gives some extra support."

"Oh." She patted the big gray's shoulder again, rewarded by an explosive snort that blew horse snot all over her jeans.

"You've been initiated." Jack was frankly laughing and, reluctantly, she had to join in. "Welcome to the world of laundry every day."

Chapter Seven

Marjorie was glad to have the RV fridge that year. As winter set in and their dilapidated power lines failed, many of them impaled by falling trees, power came and went. The rural road crew struggled to clear their roads, Blue had to bulldoze his way through drifts to pee, and when she saw Jack he was usually plowing snow. Without being asked, he cleared behind her car enough for her to get out of her driveway so she could risk her life driving to work, and she kept meaning to thank him, but then it was Christmas and he disappeared.

She had nowhere to go. Her mother had personified drug abuse before it became a thing, finally overdosing on booze and diet pills in what everyone hoped was an accident. Marjorie had never been sure. The loss had helped propel her into a helping profession, but after funding her education, her father had retired to Florida, thinking she was safely married to Jeff. And she had been, for eight years. Now she wasn't. The only safety she had was whatever she could make for herself.

Daddy would have sent her money for a plane ticket, but there was Blue. Boarding him would cost as much as the ticket and her Dad was with his friend Sophie, a widow who lived with him but wouldn't marry him.

Marjorie settled for a long Skype session with him, gifts sent and received, and a prime rib and Yorkshire pudding for herself and Blue. She didn't bother with a tree, knowing the pup would probably water it in exactly the way she didn't want. Maybe next year, she thought.

There wasn't a peep over at Jack's, his truck was gone and she was starting to worry about the horses when she saw another truck pull in where his usually was. A young man in jeans, boots and parka got out, headed for the barn. It was probably OK, she thought...probably. Pulling on her own boots and parka, she called her dog and went to check out who was at Jack's house, because she knew darn well he wasn't.

The barn door was open, the lights were on, and a young red-haired kid who looked like he might be one of Jack's students was mucking out poop from Oliver and his stablemate, both of them warmly blanketed and eating hay from full nets tied in the corners of their stalls.

"Hi," she called. "Who are you?"

"I'm Ralph. You the neighbor?"

"Yes," she said cautiously, with a faint note of inquiry.

"Yeah, Jack was afraid I'd freak you out. Sorry."

"Where is he?"

"Idaho."

"Idaho?"

Ralph had stopped shoveling, looking at her in a friendly enough way. "Yeah, his father lives out there. He usually sees him at Christmas. I'll be taking care of the horses until he gets back."

"Oh...uh...sure." It was none of her business, of course. But...Idaho?

"It'll be about a week, depending on if he stops to see his Mom."

"Where is she?" She couldn't resist asking

"Vegas."

Wow. There had to be a story there, but wasn't hers just as odd? He'd be back. At one time, she would have been thrilled to have him disappear. Now, she worried about his horses.

"OK," she said. "I just thought I'd check who's here."

Ralph started shoveling again. "No problem."

Summarily dismissed by a manure fork, she headed back to the house, trailed by her dog. She was so disgruntled she forgot to see if he had grabbed some warm, tasty manure as usual and they had a momentary tussle on the porch as she fought to keep him from taking it inside. She won at a cost to her gloves and stomped into the house throwing them down the basement steps to the daily load of laundry Jack had warned her she'd have if she hung around horses.

* * * *

Blue had finally graduated to sleeping in the bed with her, since he could last through the night. She was relieved, because a fifty-pound dog on top of her in the recliner was getting uncomfortable. She was just dozing on New Year's Eve, planning on roasting pork in the morning because everybody—everybody—ate pork and sauerkraut on New Year's Day. It was like religion.

Suddenly Blue stood upright, using her as a step to peer out the window in her small dressing room. It fronted directly on Jack's driveway and Blue's tail began going like a rotor just as she saw the sweep of headlights. Apparently, judging by the dog's reaction, he was back. She grunted as Blue launched himself, using her as a springboard, half falling down the steps like an animated, parti-colored bowling ball. He was headed for the back door and would practically knock it off the hinges if she didn't let him out, so she dragged herself out of bed to let him in the yard so he could see the object of his adoration.

It was Jack, disclosed by her floodlights and his own, which were motion-activated. Silhouetted against the snow, he turned at the sound of Blue roaring like a lion, leaping at the fence. Fortunately, the dog's legs were too short and his center of gravity too low for him to ever make it over, but he was giving it his best shot.

"Hey, Bluie," he called. "It's all right, it's just me."

"Yeah, we know," Marjorie muttered. Inelegantly clad in a

heavy flannel robe and the ubiquitous Bean boots, she waved briefly at Jack while guarding her dog. It was probably unnecessary, she thought. Blue was rapidly approaching the point at which he could annihilate a coyote, fifty pounds of solid muscle and a jaw like iron.

"Hey, can I stop over for a minute in the morning?" Jack called. "Got something for you."

"Me?"

"Yeah, something for New Year's. I won't come early."

She thought maybe it was time to let Jack into her house. "OK."

Chapter Eight

It was no trick to be up early the next morning, since Blue never let her sleep in anyway. She got a pork roast in the oven early, smothered in sauerkraut and onion, caraway seed, salt and pepper. An apple pie sat on the rack below it, while she peeled potatoes to mash. A crock pot full of sauerbraten was already simmering, generously flavored with ginger snaps. If she was going German for the day, Marjorie decided, she was going all the way. She pinched out a few of the spaetzle Grandma Bruner had taught her to make, dropping them into boiling chicken broth. Christmas cookies she already had, plenty of them, the buttery pressed cookies Mom had always made and the Berlinerkranzer from Aunt Kitty. Both women were gone now, but their recipes lived on with her.

Jack had a different heritage. When she answered his knock at the door around eleven, he handed her a loaf of obviously homemade bread and a blue and white crock. Opening it, she found a bag of pink Himalayan salt.

He was watching as if to determine whether she understood, and she began to grin.

"You're the wrong color to First Foot my door," she said, "but you're tall enough. Come on in."

He laughed and came in, leaning to pet Blue, who was in transports of delight. Scotch-Irish on her father's side, Marjorie was familiar with First Footing—an old Scottish tradition that mandated a tall, dark man should be the first one over your threshold on New Year's Day, bringing you bread and salt for luck.

"I guess you only get half luck," Jack said, "but I did my best." He was very blond, after all.

"You did fine," she judged. "Half luck is better than none, right?"

"Agreed."

"We can eat this with dinner," she said, punching the loaf gently. It had a gratifying crust. "You are staying, right?"

The whole house smelled like food. Of course he was staying.

"If I'm invited." He was giving her a rather gentle look, hard to decipher. She decided he was touched.

"You are," she said. "Do you drink?"

"No."

It was said so definitely that it made her look up. She had taken him for a beer guy.

"I've got sparkling cider, non-alcoholic. Good?"

"Fine."

She poured two wine glasses while Jack sat unasked at the

small pine dining room table beneath a Santa Fe light. He filled up the tiny room, a large guy in workboots, smelling faintly of hay and liniment, with a side of motor oil. The scent of a man, she thought whimsically. It was comforting, somehow, having him there, and she thought he looked more relaxed after spending time with his father. He had spoken only once of him, but there had seemed to be a connection.

Her dining room was eclectic—dark paneling, snowy curtains, red checked tablecloth with brown earthenware dishes, and roses in the middle of the table. They were hothouse roses without scent, but cheery. There were a couple of fairie prints on the walls and a shining hardwood floor Blue's toenails were starting to scratch.

"What do you do with this beast while you eat?" Jack inquired, because Blue was already trying to nose the dishes, which weren't even filled yet.

"Chloroform."

Suddenly, Marjorie thought perhaps that remark wasn't funny. Word on the street was that Jack's previous lovelight had a problem with inhaling gas, glue and probably coke. How in the world had he gotten tied up with a screwball? But, of course, addicts were just people, too. Everybody looked for love.

She didn't know about love, but Jack was looking for food. He ate hers with real appreciation.

"Girl, you can cook," he said after a second helping.

"Thanks. I don't often, but I enjoy it."

"Obviously," he agreed. "Well, one good turn deserves another. Want to go to the Fireman's Ball with me?" The fire station held one on the 12th day of Christmas, a thank you to the volunteers.

"They're your tribe, aren't they?" she asked, stalling a little for time. Did she want to go? How much was he asking? Did he really just need somebody to bring in the door? That was fine, she could be just a friend, but she wanted to know which thing it was. She wasn't making a fool of herself over a man again.

"I guess so," he said. "I'd sign up, but I work too far from here."

All their firefighters were locals, able to quickly answer their beepers or the good old fire siren wailing away to everybody in earshot. Jack wouldn't do them much good, forty-five minutes away at Presser's.

"Sure, if you want," she said casually, not making a date of it. "Fancy dress? Is it really a ball?"

"Nah," he said. "Just something nice. I'll pick you up after the horses are fed."

Everybody else would be doing the same. No social event ever started until people had time to feed their livestock.

"How was Idaho?" Deliberately, she changed the subject,

pouring more cider.

"Big."

"Your father moved out there?"

"Yeah, this was getting too crowded for him. Lots of room in Idaho."

"And your Mom's in Vegas?" she pried gently.

"Yep, with the jerk she married. I passed on that one."

"Ooh, sorry." Maybe this was a little too personal.

"What about you?" He was paying back. "No family on the doorstep?"

"Well, not this one, anyway. Mom's dead, Dad's in Florida. Very happy down there, actually. He's got a lady friend, everything's good. I could have gone, but I stayed with Blue. It's expensive boarding him and," she smiled, "we're still bonding."

"Not much of a Christmas for you," he said.

"It wasn't bad. They give us two weeks off, so it's time to get stuff done. How's your house?"

"Pretty good," he said. "The dark paneling is all gone. You should come over."

"I bet it's really different." Probably Mrs. Clements was gone, Marjorie thought, erased by the tide of time. So would they all be, someday. People should make their time count.

She had no idea if Jack would be one of the things that impacted hers. Maybe. Maybe not. But, like Cinderella, she would go to the ball and see if the slipper fit.

* * * *

The fire house was as decorated as it ever got, with a large Christmas tree twinkling and red and green paper rings looping down from the rafters. The chairs and table were regulation institutional, but there was something of a dance floor with instruments already set up and she knew there would be a sound system. No man could resist a sound system and this was a man cave, with gleaming engines in the background, massive hoses coiled at the ready, set to go.

Some of the firemen were, too, in rubber pants, black tee shirts and suspenders, and boots in case of a call. They would just throw on jackets and helmets and roll out, but you always hoped nobody would have a fire, especially at the holidays. The people coming in the door weren't thinking about it, that was for sure. There was a crowd.

Always worried about dressing for the occasion, Marjorie saw she had gotten it right, wearing a dressy cream-colored skirt and cranberry sweater with a scarf. It was a little drafty up the knees, but enough champagne and dancing would take care of that—she'd never feel it. Jack looked better than she'd ever seen him, hair shorter because he was teaching, wearing corduroy slacks, shirt and tie and a pullover. She could almost believe he was a professor. A couple of people greeted him that way, fondly.

A few she knew, most she didn't, so mainly she just listened. It was how she'd adapted to this, her non-native habitat. You listened to people, you wore what they wore, ate what they ate, went to the same stores they did and took hospitality as offered. Pretty soon you looked indigenous, although people always knew you weren't. But being seen with Jack wasn't going to do her any harm. He was right at home yet, gratifyingly, she soon saw that she had his full attention.

Something had shifted between them. Marjorie didn't want to be the gay divorcee shagging her neighbor and, intuitively, she could sense now it wasn't what he wanted, either. If she went with Jack, it was going to be serious, maybe even marriage. Finally, on the dance floor, they got it together.

He was tall, she was small, but they fit. Most importantly, most crucially, she liked how he held her...how he touched her. She finally let herself relax, head against his shoulder, his hand warm in the small of her back, guiding her where he wanted her to go. He'd been doing that all along, she realized. The die was cast. She wanted this man.

"What are we doing, Jack?" she asked softly, minutes into a slow dance. It was a good band, rowdy at times, soothing at others, with the lights lowered as appropriate, giving a sense of intimacy in a fire house. Not bad, guys, she thought—not bad at all.

"Whatever we want," he replied. He looked down at her, moving her slowly in time to the music. "What do you want?"

"You, I think." She smiled at him. "You ask me here to seduce me?"

"Hopefully."

"Then we should probably leave early."

Chapter Nine

She had no sooner said it than there was a blare from the speakers she could feel through her body. A blare, a crackle, and then fire house gibberish, but she didn't have to understand to know what it was.

"Holy shit," one of the firemen said. Dancing with his wife, rubber boots and all, he looked over at the two of them.

"It's everybody," he said to Jack. "Want to go to a fire?"

"Come on," Jack replied, grabbing her hand. People were running for the door, stopping only long enough to get their coats.

"Is he serious?" she gasped, shrugging into hers as Jack lifted it up her back. "What are you going to do at a fire?"

"Couple hoses, probably," Jack said. "Let's go."

She didn't bother to ask if he had done this before. They were out the door, under the stars, running for his truck. Helping her the long way up, he slammed the door and vaulted in beside her. "It's Tony Morelli's."

She just groaned. Of course, Tony Morelli's. He'd probably torched it himself. She had Tony pegged as bipolar. Not a bad guy, but wouldn't comply with medication, wouldn't or couldn't work, probably dealing drugs, living in a place that was an accident waiting to happen. It had burned once, people thought for the insurance, and apparently now it was going up again.

It was a bizarre scene, traveling as fast as icy roads permitted behind screaming fire engines with what looked like half the township following.

"Forget the hoses, they're going to need traffic control," she shouted to Jack above the noise.

He nodded. "Maybe."

They could see the blaze the moment they turned the corner onto Tony's road.

"Holy shit," Jack said, echoing his friend. "This is for real." Wheeling hard, he pulled his truck into an open field and they jumped out. Engines were ahead of them, parked on the road with men unreeling hoses from the pumper. There were no fire hydrants in the country. Once that water was gone, they would pump from a creek, pond, quarry. Jack really might be coupling hoses, at least until tankers from the neighboring communities arrived. They would all come for a structure fire.

She could hear the fire, literally roaring, and then above that somebody screaming. Fearful that they were inside, she was almost relieved to see crazy Tony running down the middle of the road.

"DON'T GO IN!" he was screaming. "There's ammo!"

Tony was a gun nut. That place was probably packed.

"Stay back," Jack said, yanking her wrist, forcing her to a

stop. "It's going to blow."

"Where are you going?" she shouted, but he was already gone, sprinting up the road. The idiot was running toward a burning house, one he had just told her was going to blow up. Even the owner didn't want them to go in. What was he doing?

Fire was torching through the roof, tunneling through the windows, licking towards the neighboring houses. Homes were close here. She could see somebody pulling trash dumpsters out of the alley between Tony's house and the neighbor. They were melting. She had been watching *Game of Thrones* on her vacation and the only thing she could think as she watched gray guck flowing down the sides was that it looked like dragon vomit.

There were people everywhere, neighbors fleeing their homes, firemen, police—it looked like the whole world was there, silhouetted in ghastly relief by fire light. And Tony, sobbing as he watched his house burn down. She couldn't find Jack, so she went to see if she could help Tony.

Somebody had wrapped a blanket around the little man, who had the ashen, wide-eyed look of someone in shock. He might be the local crazy, but he was one of theirs. EMT's were trying to convince him to get in an ambulance.

Marjorie just nodded to them, inserting herself in the practiced manner of someone who was in charge—graciously but immovably.

"Tony," she said, "I'm Marjorie. I'm a social worker. If you'll let these gentlemen help you, I'll get in touch with the Salvation Army and they'll meet you at the hospital, give you a voucher for housing, just help you out." Hopefully somebody would also get him psychiatric meds, but that wasn't her call.

"But my dogs!" he protested. He looked ghastly, beard-stubbled and smoke-stained.

"You have dogs in there?"

Tony nodded while her heart sank. Now she knew where Jack was.

"We'll find them, I promise," she said. "If they're OK, we'll give them to Helen Morgan. You know Helen? She runs the rescue."

Most people did, and Tony nodded.

"I got my own dog from her," she told him, hand on his shoulder. This guy needed comfort—needed it badly. And the EMTs, watching him trust a woman more, weren't interfering. It happened, sometimes. A lot, actually.

"We'll get your dogs," she promised. "Go take care of yourself so you can take care of them. All this—" she gestured at the house, "can come later."

Even as she spoke, the first fusillade went up, shaking the street. She swallowed back terror. The client came first—the client always came first. Even with the bombs bursting in air.

"Go on, Tony," she said. "Get out of here. I'll check in on you later, OK? We'll get you through this."

Muttering something unintelligible, he took the first step up, boosted by the medics now that he was willing. They couldn't touch him, otherwise, and that was why she had stepped in. She breathed a sigh of relief, then gave way to terror. Knees shaking, she turned to walk to the house.

They wouldn't let her pass, but finally through the commotion she saw Jack, walking towards her with a dog under each arm. They were chihuahuas. She stared at him, starting to laugh. Tony Morelli, who kept enough guns to start a war, had chi's.

"Here." Jack offloaded the trembling dogs into her arms. He was soot-stained and disheveled and she didn't ask if he'd been in the house. Predictably, it was blowing up with great booms and lesser tremors while the fire fighters frantically hosed down surrounding houses, trying to keep them from catching

"They were in the yard," he said. "Just scared. And cold. Put them in the truck. You have Helen's number?"

"In my cell, in the truck."

Jack nodded. "See if she'll take them. We'll drive them over. Nothing more to do here."

"Aww, come on, guys." Kissing the tops of their heads, which she could feel shaking, Marjorie bundled the two little chi's in her arms. Their terrified eyes glowed like beacons in the dark.

Jack held the door for her, closing it once she and the dogs had shelter. Climbing in the other side, he reached to crank up the heater, then turned to look through the rear window at the scene of chaos behind them. The once-empty field was ringed by fire trucks from everywhere, while the road was clogged with vehicles and gawkers. Downshifting, he put the truck in low gear and four-wheel drive, heading away from the road, across the fields to the road where they had turned. Marjorie held the dogs, white-knuckled with tension, glad he was at the wheel. She just wanted to go home. The only question was, which one?

Bouncing back onto St. Swithin's Road, Jack stepped on the gas, cutting expertly over the back roads to Helen's rutted downhill gravel driveway as Marjorie comforted the dogs. Why did people with dogs always have lousy driveways, she wondered. Well, because they didn't have money to fix them. Same for horse people.

Helen met them at the bottom, hair in curlers. "Jeez," she said, "I thought Tony would have shepherds, at least. He OK?"

"He will be. House is totaled, though."

"Do you think he set it?"

"Not this time," Jack said. "He would have just torched the porch and gotten a check, like he did before."

"Then at least he probably won't go to jail." Helen handed

the dogs to her son, a tall little boy whose father had married someone whose life wasn't dogs. "Crate them and give them some water. Thanks, hon."

She turned back, pointing to Jack's clothes. "Were you inside?"

"No," he said, with a sideways look at Marjorie. "It was just smoky in the yard."

"It was blowing up in the yard," Marjorie said, tightly. "Come on, Jack. We're going home. Thanks, Helen."

She saw Helen's smirk, but didn't respond. The whole neighborhood would know in twenty-four hours, tops, that she was with Jack. She might as well be. She wanted to be.

They went to her house because Blue was there, and let him out and then in again, and threw their soot-stained clothes down her basement steps to be laundry. Then they squeezed together into her tiny shower with the cracked plaster, then into her bed, which fortunately wasn't tiny, although they had to make Blue give up his squatter's rights. He settled on his dog bed with a martyred sigh and then Jack Calloway showed Marjorie what it was to love a woman.

Chapter Ten

They held off until spring so that their friends wouldn't freeze, and then the same spot that had hosted Jack's barn raising held their wedding. The same crowd of Dutch, neighbors and friends, plus co-workers, firemen, township officials—basically, everyone—had tables and chairs this time, but otherwise things looked much the same. This time there was booze. The Dutch just ignored it, but you couldn't have a wedding without champagne. And a Justice of the Peace.

The two horses everyone had dubbed the Wounded Warriors were interested observers over their pasture fence, while Marjorie tried without success to get Blue to be their ring bearer. Giving up after he tried to swallow the ring, they simply took their vows under a trellis friends had decorated with wildflowers because roses were too expensive. They weren't going to have any money, at least until Marjorie sold her cabin, and they couldn't sell it yet because Jack's parents and Daddy and Sophie were in it for the duration, co-existing with polite smiles.

Jack's father, Charlie, was an ace. It was Charlie, wiring flowers onto the trellis, who had told her a few things in the privacy of early morning. She had taken him a cup of coffee, grateful for his help.

"Thanks, honey," he had said, reaching down from his stepladder, sipping and then putting the cup on the paint shelf. He smiled at her. "You're going to take good care of Jack, I can see that." He hesitated, as if considering his next words. But even on short acquaintance, Marjorie had realized that although Charlie didn't say much, it was wise to listen when he did. "Sweetheart, I have to tell you, I'm glad it's you," he said.

Marjorie just looked at him questioningly.

"Not Jenny, I mean. Nice girl, heart as big as Texas. I had nothing against her, mind you, except she had a drug problem the size of Texas, too."

"I gathered something of the sort," Marjorie said.

"Not just drugs. Alcohol, too. She covered it up pretty good for a while, but eventually it all came out. Jack said much about it?"

She shook her head.

"Well, it's between you, but I just wanted to say...it was tough. He loved her, but not the way he loves you. I would have worried the rest of my life if he had married Jenny, but not you. You're going to be good for him."

"I hope so," she whispered, touched.

"I know so. When he came out to see me at Christmas, he told me about you, and I told him to get his ass back here and marry you before somebody else did."

Marjorie laughed. "Well, it worked."

"You're a strong woman, I can tell," Charlie went on. "I wish you two all the happiness in the world. Hope you make me a granddad someday, but that's between you, too."

"Oh, that's OK," Marjorie said. "Now that's one thing we did talk about."

They had, and she had told Jack the things she thought now she hadn't even told herself. She had loved Jeff and voiced no complaints when he acquired the big job, the big house, the generous bank account. That bank account had paid for a pool, nice clothes, great vacations, new cars. She hadn't complained, not until her expectation that those things would be balanced with children had fallen flat. She had waited nearly ten years before Jeff told her the house and the job were the things he wanted. She had wasted all that time.

Jack wanted children. It was the one assurance he had given her when he proposed. He could never make her rich, never give her the things Jeff had given her, but she wouldn't be left waiting this time, unless it was because she was in her thirties now and it might be harder. But they would cross that bridge when they came to it.

"We'll see what we can do," she told Jack's father.

* * * *

In the end, it wasn't that hard. Where once the pictures of her sweet neighbor Mrs. Clement and her husband had hung, Marjorie put up pictures of her ultrasound and then the first nursery pictures of Brian, blond hair already sticking up in a little pixie spike. He was Blue's prized possession, and hers—except for Jack. She had never loved anything or anyone the way she loved Jack. She never would.

Exiled to Love

By

Jae El Foster

"There are times when being a witch can be very satisfying."
~ Elizabeth Montgomery as 'Samantha' in *Bewitched*

The vacuum cleaner did its job as Donna sat on the couch and watched. It was a little loud though and she already had a headache. With a snap of the fingers, the vacuum quieted to a low hum. She smiled, pleased with the quick transition. Still, she needed something more soothing than a vacuum's hum to help with the headache. Snapping her fingers again, Beethoven began to play throughout the house, even though there wasn't a stereo in any of the rooms for the music to come from.

She took in a fresh breath of air... smelled the room. Now that it was clean, it needed a nice scent to accompany it. She waved her hand at the coffee table before her. A magnificent arrangement of fragrant flowers appeared on it. Sniffing again, she nodded her head. That was just right... just the scent she wanted.

Aside from some very light housekeeping, it was otherwise a humdrum sort of day. She considered a domestic task like baking cookies or cooking up a nice vegetable stir fry, but both of those felt absolutely exhausting to her. Instead, she waved her hand and made the vacuum vanish. With another wave, she made a chef appear.

"Bonjour, Mademoiselle!" the chef greeted her in a pleasant tone. "What does your culinary palate wish from me today?"

"Cookies..." she said while still considering. "Chocolate chip cookies. Or..."

"*Or*, Mademoiselle?"

"Or a stir fry... vegetarian, of course. You know my rule about meat."

"Ah... but of course!" the chef enthused. "Don't eat anything that hasn't tried to eat you first!"

"After all these years, it's a rule I still highly regard." Donna shifted in her seated position and smiled. "Cookies... stir fry... anything. Whatever you feel like whipping up for me, I'm certain it will be delectable." She smiled again and snapped her fingers, making a book appear in her hand. As the chef walked into the kitchen, she began to read from where she last left off.

The book was a tawdry romance – one that she'd conjured up last week when needing something to take her mind off her own *lack* of romance. She'd not dated a guy in ages, and while she preferred to be away from their arrogant and macho ways, she missed the way they felt... the way they smelled. There was nothing she found more delicious than the scent of a man.

Sure, with a few words or the snap of her fingers, she could summon a man of her physical likings to satisfy her in most any way she desired. However, it was all a stage of magic, and although they could deliver pleasures to her body that would bring about screams loud enough to make angels cringe, they could not show her love.

Donna was absolutely *aching* to be loved. Not to be fawned over. Not to be waited on hand and foot. To be *loved*.

While her magical abilities would have made this seem like an easy solution, she couldn't simply cast a spell over a man and *make* him fall in love with her. It was against the rules. Against Witch Code. Love potions were never failsafe. They either made a man fall so in love with a person that it made him obsessive and dangerous, or they just never wore off. There was no true cure for a love potion, so even if the relationship went bad and one side felt it was over, the one who drank the potion would never be able to love another and would die of a broken heart.

The grandfather clock against the far wall chimed the twelve o'clock hour. Donna looked up from her book at it. It was Saturday, and noon on a Saturday meant only one thing.

Her mother would be *popping* in.

"Afternoon, dear!" she heard her mother's voice boom throughout the room. With it came a flash of white light. When the light faded, Tulip Mercy Sinclair stood just feet away. "I see you're still in your house robe, lounging about and eating bonbons at all hours of the day." The ancient woman who didn't look a day past fifty huffed and rolled her eyes.

"What bonbons?" Donna asked. "Do you see bonbons?"

"Your chocolate chip cookies, Mademoiselle!" the French

chef announced – albeit at the wrong moment – as he reentered the room with a tray full of freshly baked cookies. Joyously, he set the tray onto the coffee table.

Tulip crossed her arms and cocked an eyebrow at her daughter. "They may not be bonbons, but I wasn't too far off."

Looking at her chef, Donna asked him, "Couldn't you have gone with the stir fry?" Then, with a snap of her fingers, she sent him back to where she'd brought him from.

"Too lazy to bake your own cookies?" Tulip walked to the tray and took one of the cookies. Tasting it, she hummed pleasantly. "He used just the right amount of butter." Noticing the book her daughter held, she asked, "What is that? What are you reading?"

"A book," she told her and waved it at her a little.

"Is that… is that one of those trashy paperback romances?" Tulip gasped. "Full of romance and love and horses and cowboys?" She sounded astonished.

"Well… this one is about an English prince who falls in love with a poor maiden girl, but sure… it has horses."

Tulip looked far from pleased, not that Donna really cared. Her mother had never been pleased with her, and she didn't expect that to change any time soon. "You sit here *exiled* in this mortal house, in this mortal realm, and you spend it filling your head with thoughts of mortal love and mortal romance! What in the Devil's name is *wrong* with you, child?"

Donna sighed, marked her page, and made the book vanish. Leaning forward, she took a cookie from the tray. "Maybe I just want to be loved... by somebody. *Anybody*... even if it *is* a mortal."

"Nonsense!" her mother shouted in a severe tone. "You know both your father and I are incredibly fond of you."

"Fondness isn't love," she replied, but not in a tone that resonated with either anger or sadness. It was a matter-of-fact notation.

"Love is not something that witches are known for, might I remind you." Tulip finished her cookie and took a second one. "Any bit of time we spend here among the mortals, we are supposed to fill their lives with torments and horrors. You... you helped host a *church bake sale* last month!" She shuddered as she said the words and covered her mouth the moment they were said, as if she'd spoken the most horrid thing imaginable.

"It was for charity, Mom," Donna noted and crunched on her cookie. Tulip had been right about the butter. They were delicious. "I have to do *something* while I'm here. Dark Lord won't let me go home."

Tulip looked to the floor and sighed. "No... no, you can't. Not after that last stunt you pulled." Looking at her daughter again, she added, "You've still got fifty more years left on your exile."

"Fifty down," Donna shrugged, "and fifty to go. How's Daddy?"

"Still a frog," her mom said in a nonchalant way. "He refuses to apologize to Hazel McBride over insulting her tonic at the Solstice gathering last year. Remember, he complained there wasn't enough frog juice to spice it up?"

Donna chuckled. Although she hadn't been there to witness it, she remembered the story. "That's right... old Hazel turned him into a frog and was going to juice him then and there." Heartily, she laughed. "Ah... you know, you can reverse that spell, Mom."

"I know," Tulip agreed lightly, "but what's the rush?" She winked at her daughter and smiled. The smile quickly faded and a more serious look took over her face. "Anyway, I'm here because I received a response from the witches' council this morning."

Donna straightened and swallowed. She hoped for her exile to be overturned early, but by the look on her mother's face, she knew she wasn't going to receive the news she wanted.

"Well... don't leave me in suspense. What did they say?"

"They're *not* letting you off early," Tulip said in an almost stern way. "In fact, they've made an amendment to the conditions of your exile."

"An amendment?" She'd never heard of an amendment being added to an exile, especially without a hearing in front of the Dark Lord. "What kind of amendment?"

As she asked the question, a scroll appeared in her mother's hand. She watched as Tulip unrolled it and cleared her voice to read.

"For the remainder of your exile, you must live as a mortal and may not use your powers and abilities for anything, no matter how miniscule or large the act may seem. Failure to comply will cause you to be stripped of your magic forever." The scroll dematerialized as Tulip finished reading. "In other words, you must live *with* the mortals, *as* a mortal."

"*No!*" Donna shrieked in horror. "No, there must be some mistake!"

"There is no mistake, dear child," her mother told her. "Enjoy that fresh batch of cookies from your imported chef, because it's the last such batch you'll have for a long time." Tulip tilted her head and seemed to notice the music. "Beethoven must go too." She snapped her fingers and the music ended.

So many thoughts... so many fears filled Donna's mind that she couldn't make sense of any of them. With angst-ridden eyes, she looked at her mother and asked, "What will I do? For food? For... stuff?"

"It's very simple," Tulip replied, smiling again. "You'll go out and get a job! You'll shop for your food, and anything else you need. The house was supplied as a part of your exile, so you don't have to worry about being out on the street or without power or water. That, at least, should put you at ease."

All Donna got out of that was the thing about getting a job. She had no skills. She knew how to brew a mean potion and put a proper curse on a voodoo doll, but those skills weren't allowed anymore. She didn't even know how to do her own vacuuming or bake fresh cookies.

She was doomed. Of that, she was certain.

"But, Mom…" she began. Before she could finish her though, a strange beeping sound came from Tulip's wristwatch.

"Oh, dear… look at the time!" she noted as she checked her alarm and silenced it. "I'm going to be late for my massage. I simply must go."

"But, Mom!" she tried again, to no avail.

"Ta, ta!" Tulip said, smiled, and waved goodbye as she disappeared into a flash of bright light.

As the light faded away, a brown paper-wrapped package appeared on the table beside the cookies. Donna grabbed it and opened it. Within it, she found a decent amount of American money and a note. The note informed her that the refrigerator was now stocked with enough food for two weeks, and her bedroom closet had been filled with the current season's worth of appropriate mortal outfits.

Donna felt a moment of relief as she read the note. Her closet had been bare up until now. Everything she'd wanted to wear, she'd been able to conjure. The same went for food.

The rest of the note told her to spend the money wisely and to find work immediately. The note and the package of money were from her mother.

Despite this act of selfless help from Tulip, Donna realized her life was now dramatically changed. For the first time ever, if she wanted something done, she would have to do it herself.

* * * *

She savored her gourmet chocolate chip cookies until she felt bloated from them. Then, she walked upstairs to her bedroom and opened her closet. Inside, she found a mess of clothes that were appropriate for only the most prudish of women. Each item was black, white, or gray – an enormous contrast to the colorful array of garments Donna usually wore. It was the closet of a stereotypical witch, filled by a mother who wouldn't have worn even one of the outfits herself. She decided the wardrobe was her mother's idea of a joke, and she had no choice but to choose something from it to wear.

In an attempt to make her new clothes more fashionable, she mixed and matched until she'd pieced together a suitable black pantsuit with a white shirt, buttoned to the collar. She knew nothing of hair or makeup, so she pulled her hair behind her into a ponytail and left her face natural. To finish the outfit, she chose a pair of simple black shoes and pocketed some of the money Tulip gave her.

"I wonder…" she thought aloud as she started down the stairs to the front door, "what kinds of jobs are open and hiring on a Saturday?"

There were, of course, thousands of possible jobs out there. She considered what it would be like to be the CEO of a large corporation, or to be a successful fashion designer. Maybe, if she played her cards right, she could star in a motion picture or land a recording contract by dinnertime.

Those, she knew, were true possibilities for her – *if* she was able to use her powers. Without her powers, she felt pretty useless in the workplace. Then, she thought, every employed mortal must have felt useless before getting that first job. This was no different than that. They had found a use, and so would she.

She just wasn't sure where or how.

"A latte…" she mumbled as she stepped outside her home and walked to the sidewalk. "A latte would definitely help me think right."

Normally, she would have just teleported to the coffee shop of her choice – no matter where in the world it was. Now, she didn't have that option, and as she lived in a suburban neighborhood without a public transportation system, she'd have to walk.

"I'm glad I went with sensible shoes," she noted with a cringe.

As she walked, she noticed several neighbors outside, enjoying the sunny Saturday afternoon. Donna knew none of them. She never ventured on foot anywhere – especially around this neighborhood. The neighbors either waved at her, smiled, or both. With gritted teeth, she returned the gestures. Her eyes scoped the streets, the street signs, the beautiful houses and the well-groomed yards. Nowhere did she see a café.

"Latte?" she called to an old man on his porch. "Where are the lattes?"

The old man, obviously hard of hearing, waved at her and smiled.

Slowly spinning in a circle, she looked at the other random, unknown faces and asked, "Where is coffee? You know… a coffee shop? A café? Lattes? Cappuccino? I need caffeine!"

Some of the neighbors muttered amongst themselves, while others ignored her completely.

"Are these people deaf?" she whispered to herself. "Have they never heard of coffee?"

"Sure," she heard a voice answer from behind. Turning around, she stared into the large brown eyes of a young handsome man. He wore a white t-shirt that was so tight it seemed like it was painted on, and Donna heard herself gasp. "We've heard of coffee." His smile was overwhelmingly charming. It momentarily rendered her speechless. "Just most of us have never actually seen you leave your house before."

"I..." she began, trying to brush off the shock of the handsome man's sudden appearance long enough to find her words. "I... don't get out much."

"Well, yeah... that much I think we all know." He seemed to study her for a moment, gazing at her puzzled expression. Then, his broad smile widened. "Nearest coffee shop is in town – a good ten minute drive."

"Drive?" she questioned, blinking repeatedly. "Like... in a *car*?"

"Yep! Like in a car. You know... those things that go *vroom vroom* and honk and stuff."

Donna had no car. She'd had no reason to own a car. Teleporting from place to place eliminated her carbon footprint. Who would want to replace that with a car?

"I – I don't have a car..." she muttered and looked away from the man with the perfectly chiseled jaw-line.

The neighbor looked her over once more and then cocked an eyebrow. His smile never faltered. "Well, there's always Café Devon."

Again, Donna looked all around, but she still saw no coffee

shop. "How far away is this… Café Devon?"

"Right there," he said and pointed at the house that was one lot down from her own. "It doesn't offer lattes or biscotti, but it has a coffee maker, a bowl of sugar, and three different kinds of creamer."

Donna gazed at the house and then at the beautiful man before her. The afternoon sunlight shined upon his dark-colored skin.

"My name's Devon," he told her, obviously noting her confusion, "and that's my house."

"Devon…" she whispered in a way that made her feel like she was just awakening from a dream. "I – I'm Donna…"

Devon extended a hand, which Donna timidly accepted. His shake was firm – strong but not rough – and she caught herself trembling from the touch of it. Her eyes fell from his and traced down his strong neck and muscular chest to the well-formed abs that rippled against the t-shirt with every breath he took.

"It's good to finally meet you, Donna," he said in a voice that was as smooth as silk. She fidgeted in her stance. "So… how about that coffee? I'd love to chat with you… get to know you better? I have a great patio out back."

Oh, he looks delicious, she thought as she made eye contact again. "That sounds delicious," she answered.

"Well, alright!" Devon smiled and took a step back. Then,

pointing at her, he yelled to the neighbors. "Donna! Her name's Donna!"

The sound of her name being shouted threw her for a start and she clamped a hand to her chest. Wide-eyed, she looked at Devon.

"Sorry about that," he told her, letting his voice fall back to a normal pitch. "I was elected to talk to you."

"Elected?"

"Like I said, we've never really seen you come outside." He smiled again. His lips were succulent. "Come on. I'll put on a fresh pot of brew."

Eager to get off the street and away from the curious eyes of many neighbors, she let Devon lead the way. As he walked ahead of her, she watched his perfectly formed bottom flex and bulge with every step he took. She'd never seen such a perfect-looking butt on a mortal man before. It was ample and stunning. She could only imagine what it looked like without the jeans to conceal it.

He cleared his throat and she wondered if he knew she was checking out his butt. She considered reading his thoughts to find out, but then she remembered that she could no longer do that. It was a form of magic, and the new *amendment* forbade it.

On the outside, Devon's house was lovely. Within it, it was stunning, masculine, and surprisingly clean. She hadn't, by any means, expected it to be dirty. Yet, even warlocks were untidy with their surroundings, and she just figured the same went with all mortal men. This mortal proved her wrong.

"Welcome to my humble abode," he told her as he shut the door behind them. "I hope your palate is ready for the most scrumptious cup of home-brewed coffee you've ever drank."

She smiled, put at ease by his kindness and the natural sense of humor that showed with his words. "Thank you," she said as she looked around, slowly following him through the living room and into the kitchen. The living room was darkly decorated, with brown leather furniture, plum colored walls, and a brick fireplace that took up most of one wall. Paintings by different artists filled the rest of the wall space. Each offered an array of color to help brighten the room and add depth.

The kitchen, on the other hand, was the brightest, most sterile looking one she'd ever seen. The floor looked so clean she thought she could lap up spilled milk from it. All of the appliances were shiny steel, and the countertop and island were granite. It was stunning and looked incredibly expensive.

As Devon went to the coffeemaker to begin the fresh pot, Donna took a seat at a small table by a sliding glass door. She gazed out the window to the fenced backyard and noticed the patio set he'd earlier mentioned. It was pretty, she thought, but not nearly as much so as her host.

"So, as the unofficial welcoming committee of the Savory Falls neighborhood," Devon said as he turned the coffeemaker on and faced her again, "welcome! If not to the neighborhood, then at least welcome out of your house."

He smiled wide and so did she. She wondered if she was blushing. "Thank you," she told him and averted her eyes to the table. "It's... been a hectic day."

Devon took two mugs from a cupboard and set them on the counter. "Hectic? The way you were hunting caffeine, I figured you're on a deadline or something."

"Or something..." she noted and nodded her head. She couldn't possibly tell him the truth of what was happening. He'd laugh her right back out the door. Yet, she didn't feel like she should lie either. "My... financial situation has changed. I have to find a job."

"Uh oh," he said and began to pour the first drops of coffee. "I recognize that tone in your voice. Who in their right mind would break up with a beautiful woman like you?"

He called me beautiful! she squealed in her thoughts. Composing her excitement over the compliment, she took a breath and answered. "No... that would have required me to have been in a relationship to begin with." She noticed his smile grow just a little at that information. "Let's just say my inheritance has run out."

He said nothing for a moment as he retrieved the creamers and the bowl of sugar. He set them on the table and then carried over the two cups of steaming coffee. "Did you inherit that house?" he asked and sat across from her.

Nodding her head, she added two spoonfuls of sugar to her coffee. "Yes," she told him and poured in a little plain cream. "It's been in the family since it was built."

"I bought this one flat out about ten years ago, right after they built it." He kept his coffee black, blew on it, and sipped. "Of course, most of my family is still alive and kicking, so I haven't really had a chance to inherit anything yet." He chuckled lightly as if he'd said the wrong thing. "I mean… I don't really plan on inheriting anything. I hope everyone lives to be a thousand, you know what I mean?"

"It's been known to happen," she noted and sipped the coffee. It wasn't a latte, but it was caffeine at least. She smiled as she swallowed.

"So, what kind of work are you looking for?" His question came fast. She still didn't know how to answer it – not even for herself.

With a groan, she slumped a little in her seat. "I have no idea," she admitted. The words were like acid to her. While witches did, indeed, work, they didn't do the same types of work that mortals did.

"Well... do you have any skills?"

Suddenly, she felt like she was on a job interview instead of having coffee at a neighbor's house. Looking at him over the rim of the mug, she said, "None whatsoever," and sipped.

Devon chuckled a bit and relaxed. He shook his head at her as he drank his black-as-night brew. Suddenly, he sighed and set his cup down. "You're gonna have a time trying to find work with *those* skills," he told her and made a *tsking* sound.

She laughed. A quick *hah!* He was telling her nothing she didn't already know. The only difference was that he was telling her this over a hot cup of coffee. For that much, at least, she was thankful. "All I'm good for is running up a tab and dancing the night away." Shrugging, she sipped again.

Devon's eyebrows rose. His smile reappeared. He was looking at her strangely, and as handsome as he was, it made her cringe.

"What?" she asked, averting his eyes and looking at her coffee.

"You can dance?" he questioned. His tone changed.

"It's what I do best," she admitted. "I'm trained in everything from salsa to samba to tango to ballet... If someone's looking for a dance partner, I can give them a run for their money, but that's about it."

He stared at her, eyes wide; jaw gaping. She looked at him

in wonder. Had she shocked him? Had she made herself seem like nothing but a ditsy blond who knew how to shake it on the dance floor but was otherwise worthless? There was only one mortal profession in America that she knew involved sexy women dancing, and she did not want to become a stripper. Dancing for fun was one thing. Dancing for ogling men was another.

"I know what you're thinking, and I'm not going to become a stripper," she said before he could even get the suggestion out.

"What?" he asked. His eyebrows rose again.

"Nope. I won't do it. I'm not going to take my clothes off for money, no matter how good at it you think I'll be." She folded her arms and cocked her head to the side, letting him know she was adamant about this decision.

"Hey, now... I think you have the wrong idea here, Donna," he defended. There was that chuckle again – the one that seemed slightly nervous. "Look, the *last* thing I want is for you to have to take your clothes off."

Really? she questioned in her mind. He didn't have to be so blunt about it... Donna thought she had a decent enough body. If she really, *really* wanted to become a stripper... she could pull it off.

"Wait." He blinked, as if now in a questioning thought. "That... that didn't come out right. I mean... I don't want you to think I wouldn't like to see you naked... I mean that men in general wouldn't like to see you naked… Wait… Shit." He cringed and adjusted in his seat, looking out the window and into his backyard. "Okay, I really messed all that up." Looking at her again, he clarified, "What I mean is… I'm not suggesting you become a stripper."

"Oh." She was both relieved and a little disappointed. Although stripping was something she'd never do, she at least wanted a handsome man to think she'd be good at it.

"Have you ever considered *teaching* dance?"

His questioned made her heart thump and a gasp slip from her lips. Dancing was what she did best… well, *second* best… but she'd never considered teaching it to others. Most worldly dances, she'd perfected long before Devon was even born. She knew them as well as she knew the back of her own hand.

"I – I don't have any official certifications or anything," she told him, and it was true. She'd learned each dance she knew personally from the best of the best. "But I promise I'm quite good."

He looked her over again, studying her as if he was searching for something deeper in her explanation. Devon was reading her in a way that made her feel strange and uneasy. Here in the mortal realm, Donna rarely had reason to feel uneasy, but today, it seemed like the most common feeling of all.

"What would you say if I told you I own a chain of fitness

centers?" He smiled as he spoke. His brilliant teeth marveled her.

"Well... that explains those biceps." She looked at his bulging, sexy arm muscles and the way they wore his shirtsleeve like it was a second skin. Devon smiled and glanced bashfully away. "Oh... I said that out loud, didn't I?" She blushed, having intended on only *thinking* the words, not actually saying them.

"Yes, you did," he chuckled and sipped his coffee, "but you still didn't answer my question."

She looked at him blankly. "Question...?" Then, suddenly, the memory of what they'd just been talking about rushed back to her. How easily distracted she was, simply by his damn sexy physique. "Oh... yes. A chain of fitness centers!" She smiled wide. "I would say... Good for you! You should be incredibly proud of that. It's quite an accomplishment!"

This time, Devon laughed a little more broadly. After a moment, he released a great sigh and shook his head. His smile remained, stunning and mesmerizing. "No... I'm not seeking a compliment, I promise." He laughed again, briefly. "I've been thinking about how to expand my clientele, and you just gave me the perfect idea. I've got space for dance classes in my center. Other gyms do it, so why can't I offer the same?"

Donna smiled and nodded as she considered what he told her. She had to admit, she was pretty proud to be the one that gave him the idea. She sure hoped he did well with it, but she felt like she was wasting precious time. Instead of drifting off into Devon's business venture fantasies, she needed to focus on finding a job of her own.

"I think that's a great idea!" she told him and sipped her brew. With an *ahh,* she added, "Well, I sure wish you luck with it! I'm glad to have helped with the idea." She smiled again and returned her cup to the table.

Devon huffed. He let his head flop back a little and rolled his eyes. When he looked at her again, his expression was dumbfounded. He stared at her for a moment longer and then cleared his throat. Placing his hands before him in prayer pose, he said, "I don't think you're following. I am offering *you* a job teaching dance at my fitness center."

Donna's face and mind both went blank at the same time. Then, she blinked and asked, "Huh?" It wasn't that she hadn't heard him. She was afraid she'd *misheard* him.

"I have *got* to start making this coffee stronger!" Devon exclaimed and chuckled a little more. "How about this? I will drive you down to my main center and show you the place. See if the space works for you. Give me a quick demonstration of what you can do. If I like what I see and you like what you see, we can get the ball rolling."

She still didn't believe what she was hearing. It seemed too good to be true. Here she was, banned from her powers for the first time in her life and thrown out into the world like a baby to the wolves, and here was this strong, dark, delicious man, offering her a job... Not to mention, he made coffee for her. It wasn't *great* coffee, but it was coffee. She felt suspicious over how easy this situation was going.

"Tell me," she asked him, "do you know a woman named Tulip Mercy Sinclair?" She eyeballed him, feeling this whole set-up was a product of her mother's doing. If it was, she was thankful, but she needed to know the truth before she got into this any further.

Devon grinned and cocked an eyebrow. "Tulip Mercy... what? Sinclair?" He chuckled and shook his head. "No, but damn... that's some name. Who is she? Famous dancer?"

Nope, she thought. *Not Mom's handiwork.*

"Why, yes," she lied, deciding it was the best thing to do. "I learned a lot from her in my younger years."

With a look that showed he was impressed even though he'd never heard of the woman, Devon nodded and smiled. "Sweet. So... what do you say about my offer?"

Considering the job at the fitness center and looking at the remaining coffee in her mug, she answered, "Tell you what... I'll go check out your gym, *and* I'll demonstrate my talents to you. If..."

"If?"

"If we can swing by a coffee shop on the way... I really still want that latte."

"So, it's gonna be like that, huh?" he asked, and she saw he was playing her game. She loved it when handsome men toyed back with her. "Alright. I guess my coffee's not good enough for you, so I'll get take you for one of those precious lattes you're craving so much, but, girl... Ooh, you better *kill it* on the dance floor."

Raising her arched eyebrows at the challenge, Donna stood and said, "Lead the way, strong man."

* * * *

The latte was creamy and foamy and delicious – all the things a good latte should have been. She reveled in it from the moment the drive-thru attendant passed it through the window to the moment they arrived at the fitness center. Beside her, Devon was shaking his head at her as he parked the car.

"I can't believe you ordered five shots of espresso in that thing," he said, cutting the engine. "That's enough to give a normal person a heart attack. What are you? A super woman?"

She smiled. "Damn right I am," she told him and winked.

The fitness center was called Build It Up and it was humongous. Just standing outside of it, she felt miniscule.

"This place is huge," she admitted as they walked through the parking lot toward it.

"It's the biggest of the four," he noted. "But if you think it's big outside, just wait until you see the inside."

He walked ahead of her a little and her eyes went straight to his butt. She watched it flex, wiggle, and bulge with every step he took. It looked incredibly delicious and she wanted to walk right up behind him and give his firm cheeks a good squeeze. If she wasn't on an actual job interview, she may have considered it further. Instead, she deflected her eyes from it and tried to detour her thoughts toward more important things, like what was actually going on at the moment.

Devon had been right. The inside seemed overwhelmingly larger than the outside. Aside from being ridiculously spacious, it was packed full of different areas, equipments, and people. She noticed a wall of mirrors near the treadmills and elliptical bikes. There was another similar wall near a massive weightlifting station. There were halls and doors here and there, and it felt more like a labyrinth to her than a gymnasium.

And she hadn't even *seen* the second or third floors yet.

"We have an indoor walking and jogging track," Devon told her as he began their tour. "There's an outdoor pool behind the center, as well as one inside. We offer pool aerobics and pool yoga. We also have a few very skilled massage therapists on staff, for those needing a little relaxation after their workout. There're two saunas, a smoothie bar…"

Donna thought this was beginning to feel more like a spa than a gymnasium. She tried to take in everything that this beautiful man was telling her, but there was so much to see at once – so many rooms and various offerings and *so* many people that her eyes and mind were equally boggled.

"This is like a city within a city," she muttered as she noticed an ATM beside a mani-pedi station.

"Most of the 'extras,' like the manicure station, the smoothie bar, and the merchandise shop, close at seven. Everything else is open twenty-four hours," Devon noted. "Don't be overwhelmed by it though. Like I said, this is the largest of my properties. The rest of them focus solely on the working out aspect."

"But… *manicures*?" she questioned in a baffled tone.

"We added that in after one of our *wealthier* female clients chipped a nail on the free weights. You should have *seen* her meltdown! It was ridiculous. I did a little research, found several other fitness centers in the country offered manicure stations for that very reason, and decided it would be worth the investment."

She watched him as he talked to her, but her focus wasn't on his words. She was gazing into his dark and tranquil eyes – eyes that could have pulled her into them and bathed her in a sea of lust if she stared too long. Blinking, she looked away and toward a glass door near one of the mirrored walls.

Devon followed her stare. "That's the space I want to show you," he said and led the way.

They stepped through the door into a room with mirrors encompassing all wall space. The floors were hardwoods, and there were a few yoga balls, rolled mats, light weights, jump ropes, and medicine balls along the far wall. Currently, a woman dressed in pink leggings and a white t-shirt – sporting the center's logo – led a group of seven or eight women through some stretching exercises. The instructor acknowledged Devon with a smile, but she didn't break from her class to say anything.

Donna thought she was pretty. Skinny, nice butt, decent breasts, blond hair, and lips that had recently been plumped with injections. Even though the instructor had endured her fair share of plastic surgery – maybe *more* than her fair share – Donna could see her age and tell she was around fifty. The facelifts and collagen only partially masked it.

"Mary's our chief yoga instructor," Devon told her. "She leads four classes a week in this room and four in the pool."

"It's a good size space," Donna noted as she looked around. "What other classes do you have here?"

"Women's kickboxing and self-defense, there's a cardio dance fitness class, and a guy named Brad leads aerobics every weekday morning at six."

"So…" she muttered as she stared at the crowd, which was slowing moving from pose to pose, "you wanted a sample of my talents?"

"I didn't happen to think about class going on right now," he admitted and smiled at her. "I guess I was just excited about it."

She smiled back and shrugged. "C'est la vie," she said as nonchalantly as she could. "Perhaps another time then." Without an audition, she feared this job was toast, and it was the only job she truly believed she'd be good at. She turned to leave the room, only to feel Devon's strong hand on her shoulder, stopping her.

"If you can teach dance," he began with a hint of challenge in his tone, "then surely you don't mind demonstrating your moves in front of other people."

Donna knew she had to rise to his challenge, which normally wouldn't have been a problem. Yet, as she watched the slow moving people switch into a new pose and listened to the soft and soothing sounds of ocean winds and rushing water from the stereo, she found herself lacking inspiration. How was she supposed to cha-cha or mambo without music to drive her?

She decided then that she had no other choice but to conform and try her best. With a deep breath, she took a step away from Devon and closed her eyes. Imagining herself on a tropical beach with the scent of coconut wafting all around her, she sought her inspiration. She thought of cabana boys and bongo drums. She thought of hula skirts and flower head-wreaths. She even thought of an old instructor that had taught her the basics of a samba, barefoot and in the sand. There had been no music that day, and she realized that she didn't need it now.

She only needed a beat. That beat was created in her head, thumping in time to a count of four. On the third repeat of this beat, she began to lightly bounce, lifting up and down with gentle ease on one heel... both heels... her knees and hips until she had found her proper samba bounce. Keeping that bounce to the steady beat was the most difficult part of the dance, and the samba had always been her favorite dance because of it. Not everyone could master the samba. Thankful, she wasn't merely everyone.

With her samba rhythm established, she began a series of simple samba side-steps that demonstrated the appropriate hip motions, knee lifts, and toe-heel placements. With her eyes open again, she locked them with those of a smiling Devon, who was taking in every move. Encouraged, Donna strutted backward like a cat and then incorporated a classic samba walk. Four steps in, she adjusted the beats in her head and switched seamlessly into a cha-cha.

"Whoa!" Devon said. His eyes were now on her hips, watching every pelvic thrust and lift from the knee that she offered him.

Sliding into a split, she threw her arms into the air and smile proudly. With a push and a bounce, she came right back up to her feet.

"Want a taste of a tango?" she asked him and flipped her hair back. "Maybe a waltz or some hip hop?"

Still grinning, Devon shook his head and asked, "You do hip hop too?"

"I was once in a Snoop Dogg video," she admitted, and it was true – although it had taken a little magic to get her the part.

"You're hired," he told her without a bit of hesitation in his voice.

Relief swept over her and Donna beamed. This was the first thing she'd ever actually earned for herself without the use of her witchy abilities. It felt good to her – really good. She looked around at the people stretching. They'd all stopped to enjoy her audition. The instructor applauded her.

"Would... uh... you care for a celebratory lunch?" Devon continued. "I know a great little diner just a few blocks away."

His question came as a surprise. Although she'd never had a job before, she imagined after being hired she would go through some sort of orientation or have to fill out some forms. That was how it was done in the movies, she thought. Perhaps that part would come later. For now, she was thrilled at the idea of spending more time with this man – a man who had just given Donna her first job, and a man who also made her heart pound harder in her chest the longer she was around him.

"Lunch sounds divine!" she exclaimed and started to walk with him toward the door.

While dancing was effortless for her, the simple act of walking seemed much more complicated right then. On her second step forward, she tripped herself and tumbled to the floor.

"I'm okay!" she exclaimed and climbed back to her feet as quickly as she could. It was true; she hadn't injured herself. Nothing more than her pride, anyway.

Devon chuckled and took her hand. Goosebumps came to her from the touch. "Where did those two left feet come from all of a sudden?" he asked as he led her to the door.

"Hey!" she remarked and cocked an eyebrow. "I said I could dance. Walking is a *lot* harder." She smiled again as he escorted her through the doorway.

* * * *

They ate at a small diner called Katt's Kitchen. Katt happened to be a friend of Devon's and ran one heck of a restaurant. The food was southern style – not the healthiest and offered the smallest list of items appropriate for a vegetarian – but Donna enjoyed what she ordered thoroughly. She'd spent so much of her life wining and dining at the ritziest restaurants in the world, not to mention ordering up private chefs at home whenever she wasn't in the mood to go out. This food was different than what she normally ate. It tasted greasy and full of calories. Still, if she was to make a career out of dancing, she knew she'd burn away the calories without a problem.

Devon ate like a mad man. He ordered the Hungry Guy Special, which consisted of three platters of fried chicken, mashed potatoes, green beans, corn, rolls, coleslaw, and freshly cut apple slices. By the time Donna had finished her one platter of food and was genuinely full, Devon was most of the way through his entire meal. She'd never seen a man in such good shape eat like he did. It was impressive, she thought. If he could eat like that and still keep that hard body, he was a true testament of what a real man could be.

They talked briefly about the fitness center and the upcoming dance classes. It was decided she would teach three types of classes – ballroom, Latin, and hip hop. She'd also teach the classes twice a week, for a total of six weekly sessions. If more people signed up, they'd add more classes.

Then, they discussed more intimate stuff, like where they were from, where they went to school, and what their favorite movies were. While Devon's information had been impressive, Donna's had been fudged. When she was schooling age, public schools didn't even exist yet. The only stuff she was honest about was her tastes in movies.

"Huh…" he muttered and raised his brow. "I didn't really picture you as a scary movie fan."

She chuckled lightly and sipped her ice water. "And I didn't picture you as the type of man who enjoyed romantic comedies," she noted.

"Oh? And what type of man would you categorize me as?"

She grinned slyly. Looking him over, she said, "Action movies. You seem like the beefy action hero type."

He smiled and shook his head. "Nah… all those explosions and shootouts. Too violent for my blood. I'm a love and peace sorta guy."

Even though she'd pinned him wrong, his response pleased her. She was about to ask him another question when she saw an all-too-familiar face walk into the diner, shoot her a glance, and then head straight to the restroom.

With a sigh, Donna cleared her throat and began to stand. "Can you excuse me for a moment? I just need to… powder my nose."

"Of course!" he replied. "Take your time. I think I'm going to order pie. You want pie?"

She thought it over and nodded her head. "Pie sounds delicious. Anything with fruit, if they have it."

"Katt makes a damn good cherry pie," he noted.

With that, Donna left the table and walked to the restroom. Inside, she found her mother awaiting her at the sinks. Tulip was checking her make-up in the mirror, but Donna didn't know why. Her make-up was *always* flawless.

"Mom!" she exclaimed in a hushed tone as she walked up to the woman. "What are you doing here?"

Tulip turned to face her and asked, "Shouldn't I be asking you the same thing? You're supposed to be finding employment, dear. Not hitting on men… no matter how handsome they may be."

Donna's expression lightened. "So, you saw him?"

"He's *delicious.*" Tulip licked her lips like a cat in heat. "Still, you need to adjust to your mortal life, and that means finding mortal work. There is *no* time to waste."

Grinning, Donna realized she had the upper hand in this conversation. "For your information, I *have* found work."

"You have?" Tulip sounded as shocked as she suddenly looked.

"Yep. And that tall, dark and handsome man at that table… he's my new boss." She smirked and adjusted her stance in a way that dared her mother to find a flaw with the situation.

Tulip stared at her for a moment and then burst into cackling laughter. "Oh, Donna!" she cried out and tried to calm her tone. "There hasn't been a prostitute in our family for generations!

I know things are hard, but you don't have to whore yourself out to make ends meet. Surely, you can find a nice job at a grocery store or washing dishes somewhere."

Donna gave her mother a wicked stare as she took in what she said. Then, deciding it wasn't a good idea to combat a witch who could still use her powers, she sighed and shook her head.

"No, Mom. I'm going to teach dance lessons at that man's fitness center," she said with a teeth-gritting smile.

Tulip's eyebrows rose. "Dance lessons?" she asked first. Then, her brow wrinkled as she considered it. "That man owns a fitness center?"

Donna nodded. "Yep. Four of 'em."

Tulip's expression lightened. "Is he *single*?"

Donna eyed the old witch for a long moment before replying, "For you, no."

"No? What do you mean no?"

"You have the whole *universe* to find eligible men to play with," Donna told her in as strict a tone as she dared try. "I am limited to here, with what's available to me, and that man out there is available to *me*."

Tulip crossed her arms and looked her daughter over. After an uncomfortable moment of this, she said, "I still say you should focus your time here working and trying to better yourself. Getting caught up with a man will bring you nothing but trouble...

especially a *mortal* man."

She hated the way her mother said *mortal*. It made her skin crawl with feelings of doom.

"Regardless," Donna told her, holding firm, "you should stay away from him."

"Is that a warning?" Tulip's thin lips formed a daring smile. "I could turn you into a frog right now, you know."

"And I could turn you into the old bat that you already are, just with the wings and fangs and all." Donna blinked pleasantly as she smiled.

"You could have your powers stripped permanently for that."

"It would be worth it."

And it would have been, she briefly considered before reneging the thought.

Once more, Tulip gave her the evil eye. Then, with a tsking sound, she composed herself and put on her brightest smile. "Well... I just popped in to check on you. Seeing as you have matters... *well in hand*, I shall be on my way."

"Did I get under your leathery skin, Mom? I'm so sorry..." She wasn't sorry. There wasn't an ounce of sorry in her. Even the tone of her voice told her mother she was being sarcastic.

"One of these days when I'm dead and gone, you'll miss me," Tulip warned, "and when you do, you'll be sorry about the sarcastic tone you've often taken with me."

With a shrug, Donna said, "Maybe so, but while you're here, it's so much fun!"

Her mother looked her up and down once more and huffed. Then, with the sudden flash of white light, she was gone.

"Ugh!" Donna groaned and looked in the mirror. "I swear... every wicked witch in literature is based on that woman."

She checked her reflection in the mirror and primped her hair a little. Then, she left the restroom and returned to the table, where Devon was well into his dessert.

"Cherry pie," he told her as he took a big bite, piled with whipped cream. "Fresh from the oven."

Donna eyeballed her slice. It was humongous with more whipped cream than there was actual pie. She admitted to herself that it looked delicious. It also looked overwhelming. Still, as she settled back into her seat, she picked up her fork and cut off a bite.

The pie was still warm with the cream melting from the heat. It was absolutely delicious and just sweet enough. A lot of cherry pies were filled with more sugar than cherries, but that wasn't the case here. The whole pie was loaded and scrumptious.

"Oh, my devil..." she moaned with pleasure as she tasted, chewed, and swallowed. "That's the definition of actual *heaven*!" Eagerly, she took another bite, followed by another. Before she knew it, the slice was half gone and she was feeling its heavy weight in her gut.

"It's pretty sinful," Devon told her after swallowing down his last bite. "Katt makes the best pies… always from scratch too."

"She's an excellent baker," Donna acknowledged. Then, after a sip of water to wash it down, she added, "Seriously. She could go global with pies like this."

He chuckled and sighed. "That's a hard market," he told her. "Unless you're Patti LaBelle or Mrs. Smith, it'd be pretty tough to get a foot in the door."

"Kind of like if you were Planet Fitness or Gold's Gym?" she questioned, raising her eyebrows.

Devon looked at her for a moment and smirked. "Okay, I see where you're going with that." He paused a moment and watched her eat another bite of pie. Then, he told her, "You know, you're pretty smart for a woman who was looking for a coffee shop in the middle of a residential neighborhood."

She chuckled at the comment but couldn't dispute it. In her moment of freak-out, she *had* been hunting a barista-style latte on a street filled with brick ranches and condos. "Thank you," she answered humbly. "I'm also cute."

Devon laughed at this. "Yes, you are," he admitted. She perked from the response. "I should probably warn you before you start working for me. The men at the gym can sometimes be horndogs."

"Horndogs?"

"Oh, yeah," he continued. "I mean… a woman with your… *physique*. You're going to be a distraction for almost all of them."

"Why *almost* all?" She grinned and chewed on the end of her straw.

He folded his arms and said, "Well, some of them *are* gay. I mean… it's a gym."

Narrowing her eyes almost mischievously, Donna added, "I've been known to make a gay man's head turn a time or two."

"You could probably make the Pope rubberneck just by walking by him." He smiled but then looked down at the table, and his expression flattened. "I'm sorry. I shouldn't have said that. It's pretty unprofessional, and you *just* started working for me."

Dammit, Donna thought and sucked at the remains of her water.

"Don't worry," she said to lighten the mood. "I promise you won't be trending on Twitter in the morning."

"You're not going to 'Me Too' me?" He looked at her again, his eyes lighter and hopeful.

Donna chuckled. "Nah… there's nothing wrong with a little harmless flirting, in my opinion. After all, we *did* meet before I even knew you wanted a dance instructor."

"So… my comment wasn't out of line?"

"No more out of line than me telling you that you're one

fine looking man." She raised her eyebrows again and took a napkin to her lips.

"But..." his eyes widened, "you didn't *call* me a fine looking man."

"Maybe not, but I've thought it around a thousand times since you first offered me coffee." Wait... was she flirting with him openly now... admitting to it? She'd known this man for what... a couple of hours? Not to mention she was sober and not really on the prowl. She decided to turn it down a notch, for fear of blowing it – not just the chance with this dark stallion, but also the job. "I – I sure do appreciate everything you've done for me today, Devon. I'm excited to start classes next week."

"And I'm excited to have you," he said, then, as an afterthought, he added, "teaching class..." He fidgeted with his fingers for a moment and his eyes shifted to the clock above the register. Donna followed his stare and saw it was nearing three o'clock already. "I should probably check in on the other three centers while I'm in town. Even on a day off, I can't seem to just *not* work."

"Lunch was delicious," Donna noted and reached into her handbag for some cash. Devon stopped her.

"I paid when I ordered the pie," he said. "No way was I going to let you buy your own meal today. This was my treat... as an employer."

The way he said employer made the word sound sad. The moment of flirting was gone, and this stud in front of her was now in a professional mode – one that Donna didn't much care for. She liked the loose-lipped and flirtatious Devon. Still, she understood and smiled at him as she stood from her seat.

"Can I drive you home?" he asked, standing with her.

"No..." She sighed but still held her grin. "You've got some work to do and I'm more than capable of getting a cab. Besides, I have a few errands I need to run." She didn't. Not a single one. "We're neighbors though, so I'm sure I'll see you before my first day at the center." She wanted to leave it on a high note so that they both felt the best they could about this encounter.

"Speaking of which..." he paused as if trying to decide if he really wanted to say what he was going to say. "I'm having a barbecue tomorrow afternoon. A lot of the neighbors will be there, as well as some of my employees and members from the fitness centers. It starts around two... if you want to come by."

She gazed at him, grinning and nodded. "Yeah..." she said. "You can count on it. Can I bring anything?"

He looked into her eyes, almost lost as she held his gaze. Then, he swallowed and said, "Only yourself."

"Easy enough." She pulled the strap of her purse over her shoulder and took a step back from the table. "Thank you, Devon, for lunch... and for the job."

"Thank you for being able to dance." His smile was contagious, and she swooned inside over it.

Batting her long lashes, she felt herself blush as she turned from him and started toward the door. As she walked away, she felt herself wanting to turn back and rush to him... to throw herself in his arms. Instead, she listened to the bell above the door ding as she pushed it open and stepped outside.

* * * *

For the rest of the day, she hung out at home. The cab ride back had been pricy, but she hadn't minded that too much. What she did mind was leaving Devon at that diner alone at the table. She felt like she should have accepted his offer of a ride, but even though she'd declined it, she *had* accepted the invite to the cookout.

The upcoming cookout felt bittersweet, which was a shame, she thought. She was super excited to see Devon again. She was equally excited to watch him demonstrate his barbequing skills, even if she *was* a vegetarian. However, she was worried that, even though she'd said it was okay, he would avoid flirting with her at all cost. She wished she'd never accepted that job at his fitness center. Then, she would have a fighting chance with him, but while he was concerned over saying or doing the wrong inappropriate thing, he would likely have his guard up and be his most professional with her.

That was the last thing Donna wanted. If she could still use her powers, she would have put a simple spell over him to erase his inhibitions from his mind, but this was 'new amendment' time. Her exile wouldn't allow it.

Left to her own charms and devices, she decided it best to remain professional at tomorrow's cookout. She needed the job more than she needed a lover anyway. Besides, a true, long-lasting and intimate relationship between a witch and a mortal was something that just couldn't happen. Witches aged much more slowly than mortals, and they were immune to most mortal ailments. She didn't want to fall in love and watch her other half grow old and die, with her looking like she'd barely aged a day.

The Other World wasn't any help to her either, as far as romance was concerned. No warlock in his right mind would have been caught dead being romantically involved with a witch in exile. There was a stigma attached to an exile, and witches and warlocks alike avoided that stigma and whoever was attached to it like a plague.

In the kitchen, she distracted her mind by browsing her fridge. Her mother had filled it for her when she'd filled the closet, but there was absolutely nothing in it to snack on. Every last thing in it was healthy. Donna wasn't in the mood for healthy. She was in the mood for the things all women wanted when fretting over a man. She wanted fattening, calorie-filled comfort food.

Slamming the fridge door, she took her cell phone and ordered a large pizza with as much cheese as they could fit on it. When it arrived, she devoured all but one slice – a slice saved for breakfast.

While she had a large and comfy bed upstairs, she opted for the couch and an afghan. Curling up, she turned on the television and found an old Julia Roberts movie. The film – *My Best Friend's Wedding* – was over half over and she knew how it ended, but she settled into it anyway. She felt a little like Julia at the end of the film – no Mister Right or truly happy ending for her.

This was a feeling she knew she had to get used to. Her mind was now made up that she would look at Devon only as a boss, a neighbor, and a friend. She would be Julia Roberts, and he would find a happily ever after that didn't include her. Then, when her exile was finally over, she'd get the heaven out of this mortal realm and never look back.

"Men…" she muttered as she watched the film. "They're nothing but trouble."

Donna wanted to fall asleep to the movie, but she was antsy and frustrated. She wanted to use her magic for so many things, but she couldn't. She couldn't risk losing her powers forever, but the thought was still appealing. If she lost her powers and was made mortal, she could have a relationship with Devon, and thusly, she could have her *happily ever after*. They could love one another, grow old together, and be like normal mortals in a mortal realm. No more spells or curses, no more teleporting or telepathy. No more mind reading, French chefs, endless shopping sprees, visits to tropical islands just for the sake of doing it...

There was so much to give up, but at the same time, there was so much more to gain.

Finally, as Julia Roberts faced the music and Cameron Diaz won her man, Donna's eyelids grew heavy. She let a heavy yawn release, snuggled up with her afghan and a throw pillow, and felt her eyes slip shut. A moment later, she was sound asleep.

* * * *

She woke up late and with a start. With a heavy thump, she fell off the sofa and onto the carpeted floor. It had been a sudden noise outside that woke her – something that sounded akin to an explosion. Donna sat up fast and quick, gasping for a breath. Had it only been a dream? She didn't remember dreaming, but most dreams faded away as soon as their host awoke.

There was a crashing sound this time. It wasn't an explosion, but it sounded like it was coming from her front yard. Quickly, she stood and rushed to the front door, not caring if she was still dressed in her pajamas or not. Opening the door, she stepped outside and gasped once again.

Donna couldn't believe her eyes. The house across the street from hers was ablaze with heavy, tall flames that billowed toward the sky. Stepping onto her porch, she let her eyes drift from the fire and the destroyed home it accompanied. There were no vehicles that had crashed, leading her to believe the second sound had accompanied the boom that awoke her.

The sound of sirens grew in the distance. Several neighbors were on the scene, and looking next door, she saw Devon in his chef hat and apron rushing toward the inferno. His cookout had already begun by the looks of things, but that no longer seemed to be on anyone's mind. Everyone in the neighborhood was now gathered on the street, watching the building burn.

"Help me!" she heard a child scream. Squinting to see better, she saw a little boy halfway hanging outside his second-floor bedroom window. "Someone!"

"Timmy!" one of the neighbors cried. "Oh, someone please help poor Timmy!"

Donna walked into her yard to better observe and hear.

"Where are his parents?" someone asked.

"Inside!" she heard the reply.

Donna watched for a moment and then looked for Devon again. She no longer saw him. Glancing back at the fiery two-story home, she saw him rushing to the front door. Before she could even blink, he broke his way through the door and stormed into the smoky, inflamed structure.

At that very moment, there was another loud boom, the flames rose immensely high, and part of the roof collapsed.

"Devon!" she shouted. She knew that he was in danger, and by the sounds of the sirens, she could tell they weren't close enough to help. Exile or no exile, she had to get him out of that building... alive.

Not to mention there was a child in there... and his parents. Wasn't this how she earned her exile in the first place? Her crime had been being too helpful to the mortals. Not being wicked enough. If she saw a homeless person, she made money appear in their pockets. If someone was having car trouble, she'd fix it with the snap of her fingers. Children dying in hospitals? She had the cure for that – a magical enchantment that granted a clean bill of health.

She knew beyond a shadow of a doubt that going into that building and saving the people inside would come at a great cost – the loss of her powers and a permanent banishment to the mortal realm. But... it was Devon, and whether he wanted to be all professional or not, he'd still wooed her, and she had strange lovely dovey feelings that had begun developing over him – despite her best efforts to hold them back.

"Ugh!" she grunted and cringed. "Screw it. Let them take my powers."

As quickly as she could, she hurried through her yard, crossed the street, and despite the pleas and warnings from the crowd gathered around, she rushed into the burning house.

It was so smoky inside that she could barely see or breathe. She inhaled, coughed, and felt a little woozy. This wouldn't work at all. If she didn't do something, she and everyone else in the house would become burnt toast.

"Devon!" she shouted as loudly as she could. She heard no response – only the sound of the fire as it raged all around her.

Donna straightened and waved her hand about. In a moment, the smoke cleared from around her. She was able to see and breathe again, but were the others that lucky, she wondered?

On the living room floor, she saw the parents. They were passed out – she hoped – on the ground. Rushing to them, she knelt down beside them and felt for a pulse. They were alive, even if barely. She waved her hand over them, making them vanish from her vision and knowing they were reappearing outside at a safe distance from the house. Once they were out of harm's way, she recited her health spell, ensuring they would fully recover.

There was no sign of Devon on the first floor. She blew toward the flames, causing them to die down all around her. Then, when the staircase was visible to her, she hurried up them.

Halfway up, it gave out beneath her. She began to fall, quickly held her palms out below her, and levitated upward, away from the crashing destruction. Once on the second floor, she lowered back to her feet and began to search.

"Devon!" she screamed again, but nothing had changed. The only sounds she could hear were those from the fire.

Each room she passed, she held her hand toward the door, making it fly open without being touched. Briefly, she checked inside each, finding neither the boy nor Devon.

Finally, at the end of the hallway, she discovered them. Devon was passed out on the floor, shielding the boy from the inferno that raged around them. Almost everything in this room was on fire, and the smoke was worse here than anywhere else.

She entered the room and another part of the roof collapsed. It brought down with it large and heavy chunks of the attic that dropped down onto the bed, spreading the fire and sending sparks all about. There was no time to waste.

"Devon!" she cried and rushed to him. Touching behind his ear, she felt his pulse. It wasn't as weak as the parents', but it was still weak. When she touched him, he looked briefly at her and then passed out again.

Donna performed the same transportation and wellness spells on the boy that she'd used on his parents. As he dematerialized, Devon's body thumped down the rest of the way to the floor. Donna then shielded Devon with her body and whispered a special enchantment – one that materialized them in her living room, with him lying on the couch. She was about to perform the wellness spell on him when he began to cough and stir.

"Oh, Devon," she whispered and gazed into his fluttering, opening eyes. She knew she sounded emotional, but she couldn't help it. She'd been terrified of losing him, and now that he was safe, she felt her emotions toward him grow stronger.

He looked at her with a state of confusion gripping his face. Then, hoarsely, he whispered, "Donna?"

Devon coughed again. A little blood came out with it. She looked at his body. Without the flames and smoke to blind her, she saw that he was pretty badly burned and injured and it looked like something had stabbed him on the side. Blood soaked through his shirt and 'Kiss the Cook' apron.

"No," she whimpered and fought back her emotions. She had to focus. She couldn't let him die. "With a will, there is a way," she began, waving her hand over him. "In this way, your health shall stay. Be revived and feel the life as it takes away your bodily strife."

Devon stared at her as she chanted, and all at once, his wounds began to heal. He coughed one more time, but there was no blood in it now. Her spell had worked, and he would live.

"Donna..." he told her as his voice returned to normal.

"You – you saved me."

She was about to reply when a blinding white light suddenly filled the room. She feared the visitor was her mother, but when she turned around to look, she saw she was grossly mistaken. The visitors were the three heads of the witches' council, and neither the two head warlocks nor the head witch looked pleased.

"Crap…" she muttered and stood upright. Devon began to stand also, but she motioned for him to remain on the couch. Putting on her brightest, biggest smile, she looked at the council and said, "Hi there! Would anyone like a drink?"

The council heads looked at one another and then to Donna and sneered.

"Belladonna Juniper Sinclair," Ezekiel – the eldest of all warlocks – began, "you are in violation of the terms of your exile and must now stand before the Dark Lord for sentencing."

"Donna, what's going on?" Devon asked, standing despite her warning not to. "Who are these people?"

She looked at him and shrugged. "These are the heads of the witches' council," she told him, bluntly. "And I messed up pretty bad."

She didn't feel like she'd messed up – she felt like she was a hero – but she knew the council saw things differently. Before she could speak another word, the world around her began to fade away, replaced with the gloomy and dark interior of the Unholy Chapel.

* * * *

She took a deep breath as the Unholy Chapel materialized around her. She was nervous, but not scared. She knew the worst thing that could happen was permanent banishment to the mortal realm with the stripping of her powers. Devon was safe and alive. That was all that seemed to matter to her anymore.

Donna's breath turned into a sigh as the council appeared in the jury box. The pews in front of the judge's lectern were filled with dozens of witches and warlocks, each eager to see her face her punishment. Doing good for the mortals – helping them in even the smallest way – was unacceptable for her kind. As far as they were all concerned, Donna was a 'bad' egg that needed to be dealt with.

Gazing at those witches and warlocks, she spotted her mother, who instantly caught her eye. Tulip smiled and waved at her. Donna shot her the evil eye. In turn, her mother shrugged, admitting she was helpless over the circumstance.

"Hear ye, hear ye!" a dark and gravelly voice announced through the chapel, even though the speaker's physical appearance wasn't visible. "All rise for the dishonorable Dark Lord."

All around her, witches and warlocks alike stood and began to stomp their left foot to the floor – a form of applause for the Dark Lord's presence. Donna did not applaud. She found the entire thing ridiculous. If they were going to banish her and leave her powerless, she wished they'd just do it and get it over with.

The roar of stomping died down as the chapel's door opened with what appeared to be the force of heavy wind. Then, a black fog snaked its way through, creeping along the center aisle until it was on the platform and behind the lectern. The fog then rose up and took the shadowy form of a man. Within a moment, the youthful-looking and handsome Dark Lord's features came into full view.

Once upon a time, a much younger Donna Sinclair had held a crush over the Dark Lord. His hair was curly blond. His eyes were as blue as the sky. His skin, pale, and his body was built like that of an Adonis. His mannerisms, his way of speaking… it all created a façade of this deliciously perfect being, and Donna had lusted over him. She'd sought him out, eased her way into his desires and likings, and worked to please him, but the Dark Lord's biddings were not ever kind or pleasant. The powerful creature's desires were always gruesome and terrifying. Seeing his true nature had disturbed Donna, whose prima donna nature masked a kind soul within.

Her defiance – and in his eyes, her betrayal – toward the

Dark Lord turned their relationship bittersweet. She began intentionally fouling up any dastardly act that he'd assign her until he simply stopped showing her any attention at all. Then, these acts had been noticed as intentional by the witches' council. Instead of performing the wicked deeds she was assigned, her foul-ups had turned them into *good* deeds. Thusly, as revenge from the Dark Lord, she was exiled to the mortal realm.

She knew now that he would most certainly inflict the top punishment for such acts, refusing even the slightest leniency. That was fine with Donna. She was ready for it; she just wanted it to be over and done with.

"Ahh..." the Dark Lord smiled handsomely as he noticed her and waved her forward. "Belladonna. It's been some time since we've seen each other, my dear."

"Dark Lord," she closed her eyes and bowed, as was required when greeting the being.

"I understand that you are in violation of your exile," he continued. A scroll appeared in his hand and he opened it. "This says that you not only utilized magic after an amendment was added to your sentence forbidding you to do so, but you also used your powers for *good*." He made a tsking sound and shook his head. "Now, dear Belladonna, isn't that the sort of thing that brought about your exile to begin with?"

She studied him for a moment before responding... stared

deep into his eyes. The Dark Lord was tricky – the sneakiest of all. Every word he said had a deeper meaning than its surface showed. Every line was hypnotic and lucid. She knew she shouldn't outright admit to anything.

"I have no idea what you're talking about," she said, refusing to admit she was a do-gooder. Yet, she hadn't admitted to it during the first trial either, and the council had still found her guilty. "All I did was *accidentally* mess up a bunch of stuff you wanted me to do. You'd think if I wasn't very good at something, you'd just quit asking me to do it, but no… You just kept on and kept on." She knew she was running off at the mouth now, but she didn't really care. She knew what the outcome would be, and she'd been bottling so much hostility toward him up inside for a long time. "But you've got to be all big and mighty. 'Oh! Look at me! I'm the Dark Lord.'" Donna mimicked him in a way that no other witch had ever dared. There was an audible gasp from the crowd. The Dark Lord, himself, remained smiling and unflinching. "Bad, bad, bad! Gotta do bad! And *why*?"

She looked at the crowd behind her and stared at each and every one of them. Tulip averted her eyes and slid down in her pew, looking anywhere but at her daughter.

"I don't mind doing bad when it makes sense," she continued, facing her former crush again, "but when it's bad for the sake of being bad… just for the *hell* of doing it… there's no point. There was a fire today and people were dying. I didn't do a good deed just to do it. I did a good deed because I was the only person there who could, and I stepped up. Forgive me if I don't step up to the menial tasks you give me, like making little Bobby sneeze and blow snot all over little Julie's hair in class. I'd rather have a tooth pulled than have to waste my time with stupid things like that."

Again, the crowd gasped. Their shock seemed to drive Donna, and she felt her rage toward the Dark Lord boil.

Pointing a finger to him, she walked closer to the lectern. The three council heads stood to combat her, but she threw a hand toward them, freezing them in their place.

"Don't even think it," she told them, although they couldn't move or answer her. "I'll melt you down into snow cones if I have to." Turning her attention back to the Dark Lord, she added, "Aside from all this, you've taken the wrong form. You appear all handsome and yummy and alluring, but you're really just a pig, squealing off nonsense and crapping all over everything."

Before he could blink, she snapped her fingers and turned him into a big, hairy hog. He immediately transformed himself back into his handsome form.

"How *dare* you?" he exclaimed and stepped from behind the lectern. "Perhaps an exile wasn't harsh enough punishment for you. Perhaps taking away your powers would just be petty. How about I take away something else instead?" He waved his hand to his side. Down the platform, Devon appeared in a chair, bound and muted. "You can have your freedom and keep your powers, but I shall have *him*."

Donna looked at Devon and shouted, "No!" His eyes were wide – frightened. His mouth moved, but no words could be heard. Even as he tried to stand from his chair, he was locked into place with the invisible force of the Dark Lord's spell. "Let him go! He has nothing to do with this!"

"Ah… but he does! Or, would you rather I collect the child instead? I'd much, *much* rather have this deliciously sinuous specimen for my collection, but either would make a fine addition to Hell."

She was afraid for Devon, but she was madder than Hell, if that was at all possible. Both of her hands flared out at her sides. They began to quiver and white light rose from her palms. All around, the walls of the Unholy Chapel began to shake and crackle. Those in the pews tried to stand to flee, but like the head members of the council, Donna froze them into place.

With no one to interfere, it was just her and the Dark Lord now. They were going to have it out, whether he wanted to or not.

"If you even *try* to focus on undoing this spell, I'll turn you into a hog again, and I'll keep doing it until you finally wear out," she said, spitting her words.

The Dark Lord laughed. "Child, I am *centuries* older than you. I've long ago mastered every trick in the book. There's nothing you can throw at me that I can't give back tenfold."

"You're wrong, Dark Lord," she informed him. "There is one thing that I have that you'll never have."

"Oh? And what's that?"

She smiled and said, "Hell hath *no* fury like a woman scorned."

The Dark Lord's eyes grew wide. Donna threw both hands downward, causing the ground to rumble. Then, she brought her hands together and clapped. The Dark Lord's black judge's gown transformed into white shorts and a blue and white t-shirt; a little cap appeared on his head with a spinning fan atop it. In his mouth was a pacifier, and in his hand was an abnormally large lollipop. Accompanying the outfit was 'canned' laughter booming all around, taunting and teasing his appearance.

He spat the pacifier out and shouted, "Stop this at once!"

"Sure," she said and crossed her hands over one another. His outfit changed again and he was dressed like the Easter Bunny. "Is that better? I know you have a love for fur."

In a huff, the Dark Lord shouted, "You will stop with this nonsense and do my bidding, or you will pay the price!"

"Is this more nonsensical than making someone's shoestrings cross to trip them or having a soda explode all over whoever's opening it?" For emphasis, she made a soda bottle appear right in front of him. The cap screwed off and the foamy liquid exploded all over him, drenching him.

"You *bitch* of a witch…! That's it!" He screamed in a way that nearly made the building fall apart. "You're powers are *mine*!"

"Take them!" she shouted back, although not nearly as largely as he had. "Who wants them? If I'm not witch enough for your liking, do what you want! I only performed those good deeds to get away from you. You're a… a *creep*!"

The Dark Lord silenced. He stood in the Easter Bunny costume, soaked with soda, and stared at her. His expression lightened but then his eyes turned sad. Donna watched as he became emotionally deflated.

"What do you mean you wanted to get away from me?" he asked. He was no longer yelling. "I thought you wanted to be with me. I thought we were having fun."

"Torturing people is not my idea of a good time," she said flatly.

"It's not?" He looked honestly confused. "But… you're a witch."

Donna sighed and shook her head. She'd never actually talked to him about what bothered her, and now it was all surfacing. "I *am* a witch, and if I have to give that up to appease you, I will." Her eyes went to Devon, who was watching everything with so much confusion on his face that it was nearly overwhelming to see. "But I want *him*. Or at least I want to see where it goes with him." Looking back at the Dark Lord, she added, "I just want to be happy."

The Dark Lord lowered his eyes to the floor. His outfit changed to a pair of khaki slacks and a button-down shirt, opened at the chest. "I want you to be happy," he muttered and looked at her again. "I wanted you to be happy with *me*, but if I can't make you happy..." he looked to Devon, "... and *he* does, then so be it."

"That's it?" she questioned, unable to believe her ears.

"That's it." He sighed and shrugged. "I have one condition however."

Crap, she thought. *Here we go again...* "A condition?"

"Yes... you see, the idea of a *good* witch still does not factor into this coven." He smiled and shrugged. "Give me three bad deeds a year, and you and your mortal may try to *see where it goes*," he quoted with his fingers, "without my interference."

Three bad deeds a year... she could manage that. "I accept your condition."

With her acceptance, the invisible binding around Devon gave way and he stood with a jolt. Donna rushed to him, holding him to help him keep his balance.

Looking at the Dark Lord, she said, "In fact, here's my first bad deed of the year."

"What's that?" he asked.

With a wave of the hand, she unfroze everyone and changed the Dark Lord's costume back into the bunny suit. Then, as the canned laughter returned, she winked at him and disappeared with Devon still in her arms.

"You don't play fair!" she heard him shout as she faded away.

* * * *

"Wait? What...?" Devon asked her from the comfort of her living room. "You're a *witch*? Like a real, live storybook witch?"

"Do I *look* like a storybook witch?" she questioned and batted her pretty eyes. "But yes, I'm a witch."

He took a breath. His brow creased in consideration. After a moment, he sipped the herbal tea she'd prepared for him and asked, "Like a *real* witch... spells and voodoo and all?"

"Yep!" she beamed brightly. "Cool, huh?"

He smiled. It was the first smile she'd seen on him since before the fire. "Sure, I guess..." He looked into the tea cup and swished the liquid around a little. "What's in this stuff? It's a little potent."

"Oh... just a few herbs and flower petals," she replied. "Nothing for you to worry that handsome little head about."

He grinned again and a dazed look overcame him. Suddenly, he blinked a few times, as if trying to remember something. Donna's smile grew. The tea was taking effect.

"Wow…" he muttered. His smile grew wide and excited. "I still can't believe you dragged me out of that burning house. You're a hero, Donna."

"Oh," she said with a shrug, "I couldn't let you burn up in there."

"Still… and to let me recover here with you. I just can't believe I wasn't injured, or worse."

"Nope! Not even a scratch. I got you out of there just in time, I guess." The tea's effects were in full motion now. Devon no longer had any memory of her witchy abilities or what had happened in the Unholy Chapel.

He reached across the small dining table and took her hand in his. Donna felt giddy just from his touch. "Can I ask you something?"

She held her smile and straightened her shoulders. "Anything you want."

"Would it be too forward… as your employer… to ask you out on a date sometime?"

His question made her heart thump a mile a minute. Her pulse raced so quickly she wondered if it was hunting for a finish line. "Well," she told him, "I haven't *started* working for you yet, so if we were to go out… say, tonight, we would *technically* be already dating before I *do* start."

Devon's mouth gaped a little and his eyes widened as he heard her out. Then, shaking his head, he chuckled and said, "You're a tricky witch."

"Huh?" she asked – her expression freezing from his phrase.

"I mean, you're sneaky." His smile grew and she breathed a breath of relief. "And I sure do like it. Yeah… let's go get some food and get to know one another a little better."

"So…" she asked as they stood from the table, "it's a date?"

"Oh, yeah," he agreed, nodding his head. "It's a date."

It wasn't that Donna cared if he knew she was a witch. She'd wiped his memory because of how traumatic the way he'd found out had been. When and if he learned of her powers, she wanted it to be natural, and she wanted to make sure he liked her for who she truly was – on the inside – before it happened.

He took her hand and led her to the door. Opening it, he stepped outside and held it for her as she exited. Then, as he shut it, she looked back to the house, winked one eye, and magically turned off the lights. Devon didn't notice, and hand in hand, they started off on their first real date.

The Scent of a Man

By

Jennifer Patricia O'Keeffe

"The best smell in the world is that man that you love."

~ Jennifer Aniston

She was as awkward on the dance floor as she was off it. Dancing with her two besties Melanie and Dianna, Beth felt as uncoordinated as she possibly could be. Twice already, she'd tripped over her own feet just trying to turn in a circle while pumping her fists in the air. While she was uncoordinated and thusly 'dancing-impaired,' her friends seemed to have no trouble keeping with the rhythm and staying on their feet. She was a little envious, but she really wasn't that into it. Mostly, she just wanted to get out of here. The disco scene wasn't *her* scene and she didn't enjoy it anywhere near as much as her friends.

"I'm going out for some air!" she yelled over the *thump thump thump* of the music that filled the atmosphere. Donna Summer's melodies ruled the moment.

"What?" Melanie asked, yelling.

"I'm going outside!" Beth said in a louder yell.

"Sure! We can do the *Electric Slide*!" the slightly inebriated Melanie replied and then changed up her dance moves to fit what she thought was requested. Dianna fell into the groove with her, and in a moment, the two were 'electric sliding' like it was no one's business.

Beth shook her head and gave up trying to let them know where she was going. She let them do their thing and pushed her way through the dozens of gyrating, grooving bodies that separated her from the exit. Finally reaching it, she hurried out and stepped onto the sidewalk. It was late and a little chilly out, and she was glad she'd worn a jacket. In the jacket were her cigarettes. She took one and lit it. The nicotine cruised through her, helping ease her tension.

As she stood and smoked, she looked at the people around her. Several were also enjoying cigarettes, conversations, and just some fresh air. Others were at the entrance, waiting to be let in. Across the street, people mingled from the other clubs. A man in black jeans, a black leather jacket, and a cowboy hat to match leaned against a lamppost, smoking a cigarette. Even at the late hour, he wore dark sunglasses that shielded his eyes. Beth couldn't make out much of his face, but she noticed the shadowing of whiskers around his cheeks, chin and mouth. He looked handsome and dangerous – the type of man she often lusted after but wanted nothing to do with otherwise.

With her friends inside, she considered crossing the street and making a move on him. Her flirting skills were as awkward as everything else about her, but she'd had three martinis and was yearning for a little raunchy fun.

She smiled at him and waved, wondering if he was actually watching her or if his eyes were looking elsewhere behind those shades. Excitement built in her mind as he waved back with the hand that held the cigarette. Beth straightened and tossed her curly brown locks over her shoulders. Then, flicking her cigarette to the ground, she began to strut across the street.

Horns blared. Tires screeched. The sound of someone shouting, "Watch out!" slammed through her ears and into her mind. Before she knew what hit her, she was tackled from the path of a truck that would have otherwise flattened her.

Dazed, confused, and a little shaken up, Beth focused her vision on the man that lay atop of her – shielding her from the damage he'd prevented. His skin was like milk chocolate and his eyes were wide with emotion. His lips were parted. She could see just a bit of his tongue.

"Are you okay, lady?" he asked her. His voice was concerned… sexy. She watched his tongue move as he spoke. He was sweating, likely from elevated adrenaline. It glistened from the street lights. His hair looked soft and was combed out into a small fro.

She smiled at him. "You saved me," she whispered. His lips were only a couple of inches away from hers. Lifting her head, she kissed him. It was a nice kiss… His lips against hers felt smooth as silk and tasted salty and delicious. She licked her lips as the kiss ended. He stared at her with eyes that practically screamed from confusion. "Thank you."

"You're welcome," he breathed. He seemed lost now from

the kiss. Then, as if remembering himself, he pulled off her body and stood. Once on his feet, he extended a hand and helped Beth to hers.

"I – I don't know how I could have been so careless," she said, dusting herself off. She was a little shaken up, but she was alive. For that, she was grateful. "But thanks to you, I'm okay." She glanced across the street. The sexy, dangerous looking man in the cowboy hat was gone. She looked at her hero again and added, "I'm Beth." Pleasantly, she extended her hand for a shake.

He accepted the shake and said, "Ray. You gotta be careful around here. These people don't pay any attention to the speed limit."

He was about a foot taller than her five foot four inch frame, and his build looked muscular and strong. "Yeah... so I see," she commented and snickered.

He grinned at her and gave her a curious look. "You *just* almost got hit by a truck, and you're laughing?"

"Yeah..." she muttered and shrugged it off. "It just seems like the kind of thing that would happen to me. But... I'm alive now, so I might as well laugh about it, right?"

He smiled again and nodded. "Alright. So... what were you speeding through traffic for anyway?"

Beth wasn't sure how to answer. She didn't want to tell him she was running toward a man – a stranger she'd considered messing around with just for the sake of doing it. Confessing it would have made her sound a little 'looser' than she actually was. The man in the cowboy hat had been a moment of inebriated need and want for her. If anything, this near-death experience had sobered her up.

"I thought I saw someone I knew," she fudged. "Maybe I need glasses."

"I don't know about that," Ray told her. He looked at her like he was studying something. "I'd sure hate to see anything cover your pretty eyes."

Beth blushed and giggled. It felt like he was flirting with her, and she needed a little flirting with tonight.

"Now, if you'll just use those pretty eyes to look both ways before crossing a street, you'll be just fine," he added and winked. He was so cute when he winked – especially when accompanied with that hypnotic smile he gave with it. "You sure you're not hurt? Shaken up? Concussed? Anything?"

With a slight giggle, she shook her head. "No… aside from maybe some wounded pride, I'm okay."

"Good. You want to get a cup of coffee with me?" His smile grew wide and bright. Beth grew giddy.

"Yeah," she said with a nod. "I'd like that."

"Good, 'cause I was just heading to Joey's Diner," he added. "Best coffee in town, I think. Good grub too. You hungry?"

Hmm... she thought. *Yeah, I could eat.* "Sure. I might nibble on a little something over coffee. Why not?"

"Should I get my car? I'm not sure you're up for walking." he smirked lightly.

"I *know* how to walk, brother," she defended with jest. "Just because I had a misstep doesn't mean I can't handle myself on my own two feet." With a wink of her own and a grin that showed she was teasing him, she turned to head in the direction of Joey's Diner. As she turned, she ran smack dab into a lamppost. "Well, crap..."

The hit had an audible thump, straight to her forehead, and she heard Ray gasp.

"Oh, wow!" he exclaimed from behind her. Through his shocked tone, she heard the underlay of forced back laughter. "Are – are you okay?"

Putting a hand to her forehead, she could already feel the lump forming. "Sure," she said, even though she *wasn't* sure... not at all. That one hurt, and more than just her pride. "Just fine."

She turned to face him and lowered her hand from her head. Ray looked at the wound on her forehead and gasped again. His expression showed no humor or hidden laughter behind it anymore. "Shit!" She didn't like the way he said that.

"Is... is it bad?" she asked him. He looked a little fuzzy... everything did.

"I think we should bypass the coffee," he told her as he took her arm gently into his. "I think we're going to sit you down on a bench here while I get my car. You need to have that looked at."

She felt her body flush and the world started to spin around her. "Is it *that* bad?" she asked, but she somehow felt that it was. "I – I have friends inside…"

"What are their names?" he asked her, but his words sounded like echoes and faded in and out. "Who are they?"

She opened her mouth to speak and swooned. The next thing she knew, the world around her went black and all was silent.

* * * *

When she came to, she was in a hospital room lying atop a gurney. The light was bright and it hurt to see; the walls were yellow and glimmering from the near-blinding light. Everything was still a bit blurry. She heard voices but she couldn't make heads or tails out of them. The distinct hospital smell was what had alerted her to her surroundings, and she now remembered fainting after walking into that lamppost.

"I think she's coming to," a female voice spoke. Beth could understand her, but the sound of her faded in and out like a radio on the fritz. "Please let Doctor Walters know."

"Yes, Nurse Carol," said another voice – young, male.

As her vision began to clear and the light seemed to hurt a little less, she saw the nurse lean toward her from the right of the bed. The young black woman was beautiful in her nurse's uniform. Her face was friendly; her eyes, warm and caring. She smiled as Beth noticed her.

"That's quite a hit to the head you took," Nurse Carol said in a voice that reminded her of Pam Grier. "It seems you walked right into a lamppost."

Her throat was dry and she cleared it to speak. "Yep... that's what I do." She smiled and winced from her headache. "Is it bad?"

The nurse's smile grew. "You might want to keep it bandaged for a few days. You walked right into the lamppost's *marker*."

She was confused. Perhaps it was because of the headache, but she didn't understand what the post's marker had to do with things. "What's that mean?"

Nurse Carol held back a noticeable chuckle. "Miss, those marker numbers are *raised* steel."

"Raised?" She didn't like the sound of that.

"Mmhmm..." the nurse concurred. "And, like I said, you might want to keep that forehead covered up for a while."

Beth pushed up on her hands in an attempt to sit up, but the dizziness took over again and she lowered herself back to the bed of the gurney.

"Nope, stay lying down," the nurse instructed. "You've got a pretty bad concussion there."

The concussion... a lamppost marker on her forehead... none of this sounded good. Beth cringed and tugged the sheet up to her neck.

Nurse Carol looked at a clipboard, took a pen, and marked something on the sheet attached. "Doctor Walters will be in shortly," she told Beth as she set the clipboard on the cart. "He's one of our brightest young doctors here. I think you'll like him." She winked as she said this; the doctor's name was new to Beth.

The last doctor Beth saw was a Doctor Feldman, and that was just to make sure she wasn't pregnant. "Where am I?"

"Westside Hospital," Nurse Carol said pleasantly. "Just a couple of miles from where you hit that post."

She was still on the west side of the city, and that reminded her of the club and of Melanie and Dianna. "I – I had friends waiting where I was," she muttered.

Sensing her dry throat, the nurse handed her a cup of water, from which she drank heavily.

"There are two young women in the waiting room," she told Beth as she took the cup back. "You can see them when the doctor says it's okay." She stepped back, grabbed the clipboard again, and walked toward the door. "I'm going to take this to him right now so he can look over your chart. It won't be but a moment."

Nurse Carol smiled as she opened the door. Beth returned the gesture as best she could. As the door shut, she considered her situation and how she felt about it. She was embarrassed more than anything. Literally, she was in the hospital because of her own awkward clumsiness. Did it get more pathetic than that?

She looked around the space. There was another gurney bed just a few feet down to her left. It was empty though, for which she was thankful. She didn't want to share a hospital room with anyone. It was embarrassing enough just knowing what had happened. Beth didn't want another patient to overhear all of the silly little details.

A moment later, there was a knock at the door. Then, the knob twisted and the door pushed open. Beth averted her eyes from it, ashamed and not wanting to face the doctor when he entered.

"Good morning, Ms. Houston," the male voice told her. She heard his feet as he stepped into the room. "How are you feeling?"

She huffed. A chill came over her. "Embarrassed," she admitted in a low tone. "Someone saved me from my own carelessness, and then I ended up here anyway." Briefly, she wondered what had happened to Ray. Had he called for an ambulance and then gone on his way? Part of her had enjoyed his brief company. He was handsome, well-spoken, and looked around her age.

Another part of her hoped she'd never have to see him again, so that she wouldn't have to relive that embarrassing moment. She couldn't believe she'd kissed him, but he'd saved her life. He'd earned a kiss, and it had been nice. That was a moment she'd have enjoyed reliving.

"Oh, I know," the doctor remarked. "Running out into traffic and then knocking yourself out on a lamppost... You had quite a night."

Beth smirked and glanced over at him. Then, her eyes grew and her mouth gaped. Her doctor – Doctor Walters – *was* the man who had pulled her out of traffic. Instead of street clothes, he now wore black slacks, a crisp white shirt with a black tie, and a white lab coat. He looked exquisitely handsome, and Beth felt her cheeks grow red with escalated embarrassment.

"Oh, no..." she whimpered and tried to pull the sheet up over her face. Peeking *just* over the top of it, she looked at him and said, "It's you."

"Yep," he said with a humored smile. "It's me. I was supposed to be off for the weekend, but I figured you might like a familiar face taking care of you."

"You didn't say you were a doctor."

"You didn't ask." He cocked an eyebrow and smirked. "I've looked your chart over and you'll be able to go home today, but you've got to take a few days of bed rest. No working. No exercise. Don't even do your own cooking or grocery shopping."

Beth groaned and pushed her head back into the pillow. This was the worst news possible. If she couldn't work, she couldn't pay her bills. During the day, she was the assistant manager at a clothing store. In the evenings, she waited tables. Even one extra day off from both jobs had the potential to financially cripple her.

"Is there anyone who can stay with you for a few days, or that you can stay with?"

She thought of Melanie and Dianna, but they were out of the running. Melanie was a single mother with two kids and lived at home with her parents. Dianna worked just as much as Beth did, and Beth knew she couldn't afford to take off from work either.

"No…" she muttered, hating the taste of the word as it left her mouth.

"What about your friends… Melanie and Dianna?"

She wondered how he knew their names, but then she figured a lot must have happened after she passed out. She also remembered the nurse telling her they were in the waiting room. Doctor Ray was probably keeping them up to date.

"No good," she said and shook her head. "There would be

no rest at Mel's house, and Dianna's in the same financial boat I am. She has to work."

Ray's brow crinkled in thought. "Parents? Siblings?"

"Only child," she replied. "Orphaned."

"Orphaned?" Surprise was present in his tone.

She didn't want to get into it. The way her parents died was still a sore spot with her. She shrugged and said, "Not as a child. They both died just a few years ago."

"Oh. I'm sorry to hear that." He made additional notes on the chart. "I can arrange for home-care for you. Can one of your friends stay with you for a few hours after you're released? That will give me time to get things in order."

She considered his question. It was Sunday, after all. Dianna didn't go back to work until tomorrow, and Melanie didn't work, aside from being a fulltime Mommy. Beth was surprised her parents had volunteered to babysit the kids last night. Melanie's children were nightmares.

"Sure, one of them can probably hang out for a while."

"Good." He made more notes and changed his stance.

Beth watched his face as his mind processed information. He was even more remarkably handsome under the bright light of this room than he'd been last night. In his professional clothing with his badge clipped to the outer pocket of his coat, she thought he looked like a completely different person. She didn't know what sort of job she'd expected him to have last night, but she didn't think *doctor* would have been on her lips. Perhaps a fireman… he surely had the build for it. He also looked like he could have been an actor, maybe in underground films or even those naughty sex flicks they showed at the late night cinema downtown. She could see that, but envisioning it made her smile, and smiling made her head hurt.

He cleared his throat and looked at her. She looked into his eyes and was lost in them. Suddenly, she felt sad he was seeing her in this state, and whether he'd volunteered to be her doctor or not, she was sure he now knew enough about her that he would never consider anything romantic with her. It was pointless to think lewd thoughts about him. She had to see him as a medical professional now, and maybe a friend. And he was still her hero – he'd saved her life – but he would likely never be her lover.

"I'm going to prescribe a couple of pills for you too," Doctor Ray continued. "One will help with the headaches and effects of the concussion. The other will help you rest." He studied her face again. It made her a little self-conscious. "Don't worry, Beth." He set the clipboard on the cart and then stepped to her. Taking her small hand in his large and strong one, he said, "I promise. I'll arrange for the best of the best to care for you. You won't have to worry about anything."

Except work and losing income… she thought to herself,

but still she smiled. "Thank you, Doctor Walters."

"Uh, uh…" he muttered and shook his head. "I'm still *Ray* to you. I only used a formal greeting with you when I came in to surprise you." He smiled and brightened a bit. "Were you surprised… to see me?" He released her hand and stepped back a bit.

She pushed upright a little and cocked her head to the side. He was a tricky one… she *loved* it. "Yes," she admitted, deciding it was fun to play this game. "I was very surprised. I still am. In fact, I didn't peg you *at all* for a doctor."

"Oh?" his expression changed a little as his smile grew and his eyebrows rose, making his eyes pop. "And what, do tell, *did* you peg me as?"

Beth looked at him mischievously and shrugged. "Something a little more rugged. Fireman, cop, ironsmith…"

"Ironsmith?" he questioned, confused.

"Look at those muscles." Did she really just say that? Damn concussion.

He did, indeed, look down at one of his arms and then flexed a bicep. Beth watched it bulge through his coat sleeve. He smiled and nodded his head, looking at her again. "Yeah, I can see that." He winked and stepped toward the clipboard, taking it again. "Let me go get some paperwork done so we can get you out of here, okay?"

"Okay, Doctor Ray," she replied and nodded.

"Doctor Ray…" he grumbled and opened the door, closing it after stepping from the room.

Touching her forehead, she felt the wide bandage over her wound. She again grew curious as to whatever it was Nurse Carol had been referencing. Weakly, she pulled her legs over the side of the gurney bed and pushed off onto her feet. She felt wobbly and a little dizzy from the motion, but it passed. Carefully, she stepped across the room to a sink with a mirror above it. Standing before the mirror, she peeled off the bandage.

Terror overcame her expression. She couldn't believe it… it couldn't be real. But there it was, facing her and plain as day. Red from the impact and indented into her forehead was the large number sixty-nine.

"You've *got* to be shitting me…" she told her reflection. With a nervous finger, she touched the indented numbers and winced from the pain. They were definitely there… definitely real and not a hallucination from the concussion. "Now, this is *just* my luck."

She felt a little like Prudence in *The Scarlet Letter*. Only, it wasn't an A for adultery she was wearing. It was a sex-position, spelled out in numbers for all the world to see.

"No wonder Nurse Carol told me to keep it bandaged for a few days…" she said with a groan. "I hope to *hell* this doesn't scar."

While she was up, she visited the small adjoining bathroom. When she finished in there, she walked to the window that overlooked the parking lot. The morning sun was bright and it hurt her eyes to see its light, but she squinted and dealt with it. Concussion or no concussion, she ached for a view that didn't involve a yellow wall or a table full of medical stuff. Just as she began to relax a bit, the door behind her opened.

She turned around to face it, believing it to be Ray, back already to let her go home. Instead, it was Melanie and Dianna.

"Beth!" Melanie squealed with happiness as she saw her friend up and on her own two feet. Then, her expression went to shock as she noticed her forehead. She gasped, put a hand to her heart, and took a step back. "Oh, my god!"

"Oh, that looks bad," Dianna added. "Like, really bad."

"Is... is that permanent?" Melanie looked absolutely horrified.

"I hope not," Beth said and shrugged. "It's pretty embarrassing."

"Yeah it is," Dianna agreed. "You can't go to work with that on your face."

"I can't go back to work at all for a while," she told them. "Bed rest for a few days. I have a nice concussion that the doctor seems concerned about."

At the mention of the doctor, the expressions of both friends transformed and wide smiles took over.

"Speaking of *the doctor*," Melanie began. "That's who you were with when this happened, right?"

"He's pretty cute," Dianna noted. "Like, *really* cute."

"He's my *doctor*," Beth specified. "He now knows *much* too much about me to want to date me. I can promise you that."

"You don't know that," Dianna said. "He's a doctor, but he's still a *man*."

"A *delicious* man," Melanie added. "Have you *smelled* him? He has on no cologne and his scent is still divine!" She fanned herself as she thought about it.

"Have I... *smelled* him?" Beth questioned. Then, she wondered what Melanie was doing smelling him.

"How can you miss it?" she continued. "You *can't* miss it! Honey, there is no scent greater than the scent of a man."

Beth laughed out loud. It was absurd. Unless someone was drenched in cologne or perfume, they didn't really have a scent... did they? Maybe sweat, she thought. Men were often sweaty, and sweat definitely had a scent.

"Anyway," she said, changing the subject, "he's doing some paperwork and writing out a couple of prescriptions, and then he's sending me home. Can you take me home?" She looked at them both, as they'd all ridden together to the club last night in

Dianna's car.

"Of course," Dianna said with a smile.

"Also… can someone stay with me for a couple of hours? He has to arrange for some… *home-care* for me for a few days." She sounded old when she said it, and she felt old too, even though she was nowhere near old enough to be considered old.

Melanie fidgeted and looked at Dianna. "Is it okay if I take the bus home? I really need to relieve my parents of the kids. They've got to be driving them nuts by now."

Dianna smiled and nodded. "Yep. I've got this. I have absolutely nothing else planned for today." She looked to Beth. "I hope they don't send some creepy old nurse to take care of you. They can be cruel and ruthless."

"Dianna!" Beth exclaimed. "Don't frighten me."

A moment later, Nurse Carol returned with some forms for her to sign. Melanie and Dianna left to wait for her near the checkout station. Beth felt like she was signing her life away. Finally, she was given her belongings and allowed to dress in her own clothing. Afterward, she was put in a wheelchair and pushed to the checkout, with some last minute medical advice and a notification that she'd receive a phone call before her home-care arrived.

"Great…" she muttered, still ashamed she even had to have home-care.

A handsome young man in a blue uniform pushed her to Dianna's car, where she was loaded up into the backseat, ready to be driven home.

* * * *

"Are you comfy?" Dianna asked her as she draped a quilt over Beth, who was laid out in her bed.

"As comfortable as possible, I guess," she replied.

"Good. I'm going to go into the kitchen and make us some nice tea. Would you like tea?" Dianna's smile was large and showed her eagerness to help.

"Tea would be good," she told her, "but I think I might nap."

"Do you want one of your pills?"

"Nope. I hate the way those things make me feel. I'd rather have the headache and dizziness." Beth was stubborn when it came to medication. She was clumsy enough without it, and taking pain killers or sleeping pills just made all of her awkward qualities worse.

"I'll be back in a jiff."

Dianna closed the door behind her and Beth sighed. She thought about the home-care person that would be arriving and where they would be staying. She lived in a one-bedroom apartment with a half-kitchen and a small bathroom. It was cramped enough with just her, and she sure as the dickens wasn't going to share her bedroom. Fortunately, her sofa pulled out into a bed. Maybe after a night sleeping on that thing, whoever came to help would leave and let her heal on her own.

Beth just didn't like the idea of some stranger coming in and running the show, even if she *was* unable to do a few things for herself. She surely couldn't clean. Her vacuum was heavy, and the dishes would take energy she just didn't have. If whoever was coming wanted to serve as a housekeeper and then go home at the end of the day... that sounded pretty good to her. She could deal with that. A slight smile curled up her lips as she considered it.

The telephone rang in the kitchen. It was loud and sudden, startling her and pulling the smile from her lips. The sound stopped after the second ring, meaning Dianna had answered the call. She wondered if it was the home-care people, letting her know that her nurse was on her way. Beth cringed and sank deeper beneath her covers.

A moment later, the door opened and her suspicions were confirmed.

"That was the home-care people," Dianna told her. "Your nurse is on her way."

"Great..." she muttered and shifted beneath the covers. "Dump a shot or two of alcohol in my tea and I'll be all set."

"Now, what's the worst that can happen?" her friend asked. "Sure, she could be this mammoth, mean woman who prods you with needles, ties you up, and keeps you cut off from the outside world, but the chances of that are pretty slim. More likely, she'll be a frigid old woman who likes silence and will make you take your medicine to keep you out of her hair." She smiled and held her palms up as she shrugged.

"Why are you my best friend again?" Beth huffed.

"Because you loves me," Dianna answered in a cutesy voice. "I'll go check on that tea. It should be steeped by now."

"Take your time. I'm going to lie here and see if I can become one with my bed... make it camouflage me so that mean, scary nurse can't see me."

Dianna chuckled as she stepped from the room. "You're so silly..." She shut the door behind her.

Already, Beth was getting claustrophobic. The idea of sharing her space with this stranger made her blood run cold. She didn't feel like she even *needed* home-care. Perhaps, if she became the worst patient in the world, the old bat would pack up her things and leave. She could act out like a child or a spoiled brat, really push the woman with demands and refusals of medicines and treatments, and send her running out the door.

Folding her arms, she decided that was *exactly* what she would do. While the idea came to her, there was a knock at the apartment door. She heard Dianna greet the home-care horror, but Beth caught a tinge of surprise in her tone.

She decided she wasn't going to meet this person while lying in the bed like a woman living out her final days. Carefully, she threw the covers off and sat up. Then, with as much steadiness as she could muster, she stood. The headache hit her hard again, threatening to send her right back into bed. She fought against it though, and as she stepped away from the bed, she felt that she'd won.

When arriving home, she'd changed into her comfy blue nightgown. She put her bathrobe on over it and slipped her feet into her slippers. Beth glanced at her mirror on her way to the door. The bandage over her wound covered the sixty-nine beautifully, and she wanted to keep it that way. The last thing she wanted was for this nurse to see the indention on her forehead.

Opening the door, she stepped into the short hallway and saw Dianna at the closed front door, looking off toward the dining table, which was out of Beth's view. Beth continued to walk, and as she came to the living room and looked to the table, she finally saw her helper. Her eyes grew wide in surprise. Her mouth gaped. It was Ray, dressed in slacks and a button-down. He sat at the table with his briefcase atop it. Two suitcases accompanied him at his side.

His eyes grew when he noticed her. "You shouldn't be up

and about," were the first words he told her. She had no words for him. She was speechless – surprised beyond surprise. "I thought you said she was resting?" He looked at Dianna.

"She *was*," Dianna replied, eyeballing Beth. Beth gaped between the two of them. She didn't know what to make of this situation. "Why did you get out of bed?"

"I..." she couldn't even make a full sentence; she was too dumbfounded by Ray's appearance. He wasn't a nurse – especially a home-nurse. He was a *doctor*. Doctor's sometimes made house-calls, but they didn't make them and stay – not in this day and age, anyway. Finally, more words came to her, "What are you doing here?"

Ray smiled and shrugged. "I'm your home-care," he told her. She felt her stomach sink. "It took pulling some strings, but I figured I'd already saved you once, *and* I'm your doctor now. Who better to take care of you? Besides that, I've already seen that sixty-nine on your forehead. I'm pretty sure you don't want a stranger changing that bandage." He smirked and folded his arms before him.

Looking at his suitcases again, she asked, "Are you moving in?"

"For three days, just like the form you signed agrees to." His smile was big and it dared her to counter him on this. "If you'd prefer, I can send Nurse Agnes."

"Who's Nurse Agnes?" Dianna asked before Beth could.

"She's been around since the hospital was an asylum. You'd love her. Tough as nails. Strict to the rules. She's an actual *nun*, by the way."

Beth trembled at the thought... at the description of what she imagined was the most ruthless nun-nurse of them all. Then, she wondered if this Nurse Agnes even existed. It was likely that Ray was pulling her leg. So once again, she decided to play his game.

"She sounds terrible," she told him and shuddered.

He chuckled a little in response. "Oh, she's the *worst*. They say at nighttime she turns into a bat."

"A bat?" A thin smile twisted up the corners of her lips.

"Yep. Meanest bloodsucker in the city. During the day, she's as holy as they get."

"Sounds like the premise of a really bad book," Beth replied and propped a hand on her hip.

"Actually, it is a *really* bad movie. I saw it at a theater once. Called *Bad Nun at Night*."

Beth laughed. "That sounds awful."

"Yep. It was the worst."

Out the corner of her eye, Beth saw Dianna collect her purse and keys. "I should get going. I need to pick up some groceries on my way home." She smiled at Ray. "It's good to see you again, Doctor Walters."

"Man… what's up with you all and your formalities?" he asked lightly. "Please, call me Ray."

"Okay, Ray…" Dianna grinned wider and Beth saw her blush a little as she said his name. Then, Dianna looked at her. "Call me if you need *anything*."

"I will," she replied, smiling a little but wishing her friend would stay for a bit longer – at least until she got used to having this man in her home. Another hour or two… three days, maybe.

"Trust me, she's in good hands," Ray added. "I can cook, clean, change a bandage, and even run errands if needed. There's nothing this woman could need that I can't do for her." His grin almost looked mischievous, but Beth thought she might be reading it wrong. "But please, feel free to come back and keep us company."

"I'll do that," Dianna said. Then, with a wave to him and Beth, she left.

There was a moment of quiet and it was as thick as fog. Beth looked at her doctor, still seated at the table. He was staring at her with that huge smile she adored so much. At least he wasn't some mean, horrid nurse who wanted to rule the place with an iron thumb. He was the same handsome stranger that had saved her from being splattered all across the street, and she owed him a chance. Still, it made her curious as to how he could do this.

"Don't you have patients?" she asked, thinking of his position at the hospital.

"Oh, Beth… I have all the *patience* in the world," he replied, playing on her words. He was going to be a handful; she just knew it. Ray chuckled at his joke and then cleared his throat. "Well, I have taken my patient list for the next few days and passed them onto some colleagues. I had some vacation days saved up, and the soonest the home-care department could have a nurse here was forty-eight hours. I looked at it as fate."

"Wait a minute," she said, baffled. "You're using your vacation days to sit here at my cramped apartment and take care of me?"

"Just three of them," he said and held up three fingers for emphasis. "I have eleven more where those came from."

She hoped he meant eleven more vacation days, because as far as she could see, he only had ten digits between both hands, just like she did.

"Now… where do I put my things?" he asked and motioned toward his two suitcases.

"Well… as you can see, it's a pretty small place," she exclaimed. "You'll be sleeping on the sofa bed, but I warn you; it's not the most comfortable thing in the world." Any other nurse or doctor visiting like this, she would not have given that warning. But this was Ray. She wished she had something better for him to rest on.

"Perfect!" he exclaimed and held his smile. "I love uncomfortable sofa beds. If I'm lucky, I might find some discarded change or potato chips in it."

She rolled her eyes and crossed her arms. "Clown around much?"

"Come sit with me," he beckoned instead of answering. "Your friend made tea and gave me her cup."

"Ugh…" she moaned as she started to the chair across from him. "I'd rather have coffee. I feel drained."

"Nope, no coffee for you," he informed her. "You need rest. She promised me this tea is decaf and herbal." He sipped from his cup and moaned in delight. "Just enough honey in it. That's delicious."

Settling into her seat, she blew on her tea and then sipped it. Ray was right. It was pretty good. She sipped again and set the cup on the table. "I'm sorry we never made it to Joey's Diner," she told him. "I think that would have been fun."

"Either way," he said, shrugging, "we still ended up back at your place in the long run." He chuckled again and sipped his tea.

Beth chuckled along with him. "Clever, funny man."

"I do try." He held his cup up at her in cheers and then drained the rest of the tea from within. Returning the cup to the table, he released a nice, long, "Ahh…"

Beth enjoyed another couple of sips from her cup and then decided she'd had enough. It was making her sleepier, and she was seriously considering a nap. She worried though for her company. What would he do to pass the time? There was the television, but even with the rabbit ears, the three stations the thing picked up were fuzzy and flickered. Perhaps the radio... or would he be leery of waking her?

"You look tired," he noted. "You wanna take a nap?"

Briefly, she entertained the idea of what it would be like if he joined her for the nap... curled up behind her, holding her and spooning her as she rested. She wiped the fantasy from her thoughts and said, "Yes..."

"Okay, I'll help you into bed and sort through my things. I brought a book with me that I've been aching to read ever since I bought it – months ago!" He chuckled again. She loved the way he looked when he laughed.

She was also thankful that he had something to do. Still, she offered what she had. "There's the television with its crappy reception, and the radio with its equally crappy reception." Looking at the stack of records on the table's under-shelf, she added, "Or the record player. I got a new Elvis one last week."

"You're still listening to *Elvis*?" He seemed shocked at this. "It's the disco era, baby! I could have brought my stack. I've got the Bee-Gees, some Donna Summer... Rock and Roll has taken a hiatus for a new sound and a new generation."

Seeing as they were around the same age, Beth cocked an eyebrow at the 'new generation' comment. "I'm hip," she said in rebuke. "I've even taken up roller skating."

"That's something else you won't be doing for a little bit," he said in a straight-forward tone. "I mean… I can't even *imagine* you on roller skates. I've seen you walk!"

She stood and ignored the comment. "Come tuck me in, Nurse," she told him as she walked toward the hall.

"Nurse?" he questioned and hurried to his feet. Quickly, he came up behind her and took her elbow, escorting her to her room. "I'm no nurse."

"A pretty white dress and a nice white hat and I think you'd make a lovely nurse," she teased, laughing a bit.

"Oh, who's the clown now, huh?" he asked through a smile. "You are. Funny lady."

With him at her side, holding onto her as she walked, she thought of Melanie's earlier comment in the hospital room. Then, as nonchalantly as she could, she tilted her head toward him and sniffed. He glanced at her and she turned her face back before she could tell if he had an authentic scent or not.

"Did you just sniff me?" he asked as they reached her bedroom door.

"I must be coming down with a cold," she lied and grinned.

"Pardon my sniffles."

In her bedroom, he helped her climb into bed and covered her with the blanket and sheet. Then, he towered over her, smiling down at her with his hands held behind him. "Do you need anything? Water?"

"A cigarette," she told him and pointed toward her jacket hanging on the closet doorknob. "They're in the pocket."

"Oh, no," he told her, shaking his head. "Not right now."

"Wait? What?" She was confused. Why wasn't he simply retrieving her cigarettes?

"You're in *bed*," he said with a little enthusiasm. "Do you know how dangerous smoking in bed is?"

"Smoking, period, is dangerous from what I've heard," she countered, although she didn't know if it was to her defense or against it.

"I can't tell you not to smoke because I smoke too and it would be hypocritical of me, but I don't want you to fall asleep with a cigarette between your fingers and start a fire either. So, no. You can have one after your nap, at the dining table like a person should."

Suddenly, she wondered if Nurse Agnes would have been easier to handle. Ray was proving to be as tough as he'd claimed her to be.

"Fine," she grunted and pushed her head against the pillow,

shutting her eyes and snuggling in.

"Would you like for me to read to you?" he asked and her eyes popped back open. "I'm told I have a great speaking voice."

He *did* have a great speaking voice, but she hated being read to. Before she could reply though, he picked up the book at her bedside table and looked at the cover. There was a bookmark holding her place.

"How about this one?" he continued. "It's called *Passion on the Shore*... Is this what you've been reading?"

Almost ashamed to admit she'd been enjoying a trashy romance, she bashfully whispered, "Yep."

"Alright," he said and opened up to her marked place. Then, clearing his throat, he began to read. "*His hand ran down her thigh and she trembled. The heat in her loins was too much and she felt she would crawl out of her skin. He tasted her breast and circled his tongue around her perked...*" Ray stopped before finishing the line and locked eyes with her. "Nipple..." he said in a teasingly seductive tone, letting the word drag at the end.

"Oh, my god, put the book away!" she told him and rolled over so she couldn't see him. He was right. His speaking voice was so divine that as he'd read the words, she'd began to imagine them. The last thing she needed right now was his seductive tone washing over her with the heat of pleasure and fantasy.

"*His hand dipped between her thighs and explored her*

delicate love garden," he continued, despite her plea to stop. "*She whimpered at the feeling of thumping against her tender bud…*"

"Ray!" she shouted and lifted up, pulling her pillow from behind her to hit him with.

"Okay, okay!" he exclaimed, closing the book and returning it to the table. Laughing, he said, "I always wondered what kind of women read those things."

Beth braced herself, readying her ears for the sarcasm or insult that would follow.

"I never imagined people as… beautiful as you would be the audience."

She looked up at him, suspicious, but as he shrugged, she realized he was complimenting her. He'd called her beautiful when they first met, and now, he'd said it again. She felt her own tender bud thump.

"Get some rest, Beth," he added as he stepped toward the door and opened it. "I'll check on you in an hour."

He flicked the light off and stepped from the room, mostly closing the door but leaving it open an inch or so. Beth thought about his compliment – the way he'd called her beautiful again… Warm and giddy feelings bubbled within her and she smiled again, snuggling with her covers. Shortly thereafter, she fell sound asleep.

* * * *

She awoke to the sound of water. Everything was hazy in her mind. What time was it? Was she actually in her own bed? There was that headache still, ravaging her brain like a wild animal. Her forehead hurt pretty badly too.

Perhaps it was because of the sound of water that she had to pee so badly. Feeling the now familiar rush that came with sitting up and the dizziness that accompanied standing, she balanced herself and took a breath. Then, with slow steps, she walked to her bedroom door, opened it, and stepped out.

The sound was coming from the bathroom almost right across from her. Had someone left the water running? Who was there with her again? It was hard to focus with the thumping in her skull. The bathroom door was ajar and so she touched it and gently gave it a push. As it opened, she saw she'd been mistaken. It wasn't the sink faucet she'd heard. It was the shower. The curtain was only half closed, and she remembered who was in her house as she saw Ray's muscular, firm back half standing beneath the spray of the shower.

Unable to move or turn her eyes from the sight, she watched the water run through his thick hair, down his head and neck, over his strong shoulders and sensually defined back, and finally to his tight, perfect butt. The water slid between his legs, running down them to the bathtub he stood in. As her eyes stayed focused on his rear and she took in the sudden, wonderful experience of seeing parts of him she'd only imagined, Ray began to turn around. As he did, her view changed and she saw much, *much* more of him than she'd bargained for.

Gasping, she averted her eyes and squeaked. She started to back out of the bathroom, hoping to go unnoticed, but it was too late. Ray saw her and said her name in an elevated tone.

"Beth!" he exclaimed. She looked at him again – this time, at his face. "Are you out of bed again?" He was smiling at her and making no attempt to cover his endowment. "I'll be right out," he said, still smiling, but this time he placed his washcloth over his goodies, fully obstructing them from her view. "Unless you wanna watch? Do they do that in those romance books you read?"

Before she could reply, he chuckled and closed the shower curtain. Partially amazed but fully embarrassed at what she'd just witnessed, Beth backed clumsily out of the bathroom, jarring her elbow on the doorframe as she stepped through it. She held her elbow and rubbed it, still watching the shower curtain... wondering if it would open again and if she'd get another glimpse at his oversized candy bar.

Finally, she started to come to her senses and went straight back to her bedroom. She could pee later. Right then, she didn't want to step back into that bathroom – not until Ray had some clothes on and what she saw of his had faded from her mind.

She didn't know if it would ever fade away. She'd heard

the myths…the rumors about black men and enormous endowments. She'd always laughed at them – thinking the rumors were merely exaggerated gossip. Now, she knew better. There apparently wasn't a muscle on Ray that wasn't huge and prominently defined.

With her door fully closed, she could still hear the shower water, which made sense since she'd left the bathroom door wide open in the awkward haste of her escape. The sound then went away; Ray's shower was over. She wondered what he must have thought about her – catching her standing in the doorway, checking out his delicious butt. After reciting from her reading material, she knew he must have thought of her as a bad girl… naughtier than she really was.

Then again, would that assumption have been that far off? After all, this whole mess started because she saw a hot cowboy across the street that she'd wanted to hook up with during a moment of inebriated bad judgment. Not to mention she'd kissed Ray after he saved her. Maybe she *was* a naughty girl and she was just now seeing it…

After she considered this for a bit, she heard a knock at her door. The knob twisted, and the door pushed open. Ray's head poked in.

"Hey, there," he said in an upbeat tone.

"I had to pee!" she exclaimed, instantly defending herself

in the most frantic way possible. "So bad… so bad…"

Ray chuckled and stepped fully into the room. "It's okay. Accidents happen. The bathroom's open though, unless you used the kitchen sink or something."

"Okay," she whispered in a wispy breath, unsure of what else to say. Was her embarrassment written all over her face? Did it show how impressed of his features she was?

"You napped for a few hours," he continued. This came as a surprise. She felt like she'd only slept a few minutes. "I ordered food from Joey's Diner before I got in the shower. I figured we still deserved our big greasy burgers, even if we'll be getting them as take out." He smiled at her; she smiled back. The sweetness of the gesture helped calm her. "Will you be okay by yourself for a half hour or so?"

She shrugged, knowing it would give her some time to recover from her embarrassment. "Take your time," she suggested. "I'll put on some music and relax while you're gone."

"Take it easy," he told her as he began to leave the room. "Doctor's orders."

She saluted him in the way a soldier would an officer. Then, she watched him smile and leave. A moment later, she heard him head out the front door, letting it lightly slam behind him.

"Christ…" she muttered and dragged her palm down her face. "Way to go, Beth!" she chided herself. "He's here just a few hours, and already you do probably the most embarrassing thing you could do…" She considered what she'd seen in the shower and thought it over. Then, she shrugged, "But what a thing to see…"

She had already liked Ray before spying his naked, wet goodies in the shower. She'd enjoyed his sarcasm and sense of humor. He was handsome and in great shape, and he had a pretty good job to top it all off with. Now, having been given a glimpse of what all was beneath his clothing, she found herself yearning for him even more.

"Screw the cowboy with the black hat," she said, remembering how Ray had saved her. "I've got a hero on my hands, and there's *more* than enough of him to keep me company."

With a smile, she went to the bathroom and did her business. The room was still damp with the fog from his shower. It smelled of soap and mouthwash. Folded in a neat stack atop the counter were the clothes he'd arrived in. After flushing, she walked to the stack and looked at it. Melanie's words still echoed at the back of her mind. If he truly had his own delicious scent, would it have transferred onto his freshly worn clothing?

She lifted first his shirt and brought it to her nose. Sniffing deeply, she found that it did have a scent, but it wasn't very distinct. She placed the remnants of deodorant and perhaps some aftershave. Beth set the shirt aside. Socks, slacks, and underwear remained. Sniffing the socks was absolutely out of the question.

She refused to deeply inhale the remnants of sweaty feet. Instead, her eyes shifted between the properly folded pants and the unfolded blue briefs.

"Okay, this is just perverted," she told herself as she eyed the underwear. Nonetheless, she picked the briefs up and held them in both hands. They were soft. The tag said they were all cotton, with a waist size of thirty-four.

She considered where to sniff. She didn't want to sniff the back of them. That would be too close to sniffing someone's bare bottom. Cringing, she looked at the front, at the stitched fly, and at the bulge in the fabric that remained from being worn.

Bringing them closer, she put her nose to the crotch and took in its scent. Breathing deeply, Beth found her mind overwhelmed with sudden nirvana. Her headache was gone. She wasn't dizzy from anything but ecstasy. She smelled it... most certainly... the scent of this delicious man, and it was the best scent she'd ever inhaled.

It was like cinnamon and ginger, with a little sea salt and something that just reeked of goodness thrown into the mix. There was also something else to the scent – something she couldn't place and that she knew belong distinctly to Ray. It was wonderful... mystical... it made her sway with happiness and emotional wealth.

She sniffed his underpants once more and set them back

down, holding his scent for as long as she could before she had to breathe again. Then, she shook her head and groaned.

"What the hell..." she muttered. She couldn't believe she'd just sniffed a man's worn underwear. "Ugh! What is wrong with me?"

She decided to blame the concussion, but weirdly enough, she felt great instead of worse. Whatever magic was held inside of Ray's personal scent seemed to work better on her ailments than any drug in the world. Without the headache and dizziness, she felt back to her normal self.

Spinning to leave the room, Beth felt the headache and dizziness return and had to stop and steady herself. "Well... crap."

After a moment, she carefully went to the living room and put on her new Elvis album, despite what Ray had to say about him. Then, she decided she needed to call either Melanie or Dianna and tell them what happened. She wouldn't tell them about the sniffing of the underwear though – only about catching Ray naked in the shower. They'd enjoy that a lot more than the underwear story, and they wouldn't look at her weirdly when they saw her again.

* * * *

After giving both Melanie and Dianna an earful over the earlier eyeful she'd experienced, Beth heard a car door slam outside of her apartment and knew Ray was back. The front door opened and she smiled at him, smelling the scent of food waft to her from the bags he carried. She thought about the Elvis record playing and wondered if he'd say something about it.

While he didn't comment about Elvis playing in the background, he was chatty about what the people in town were like, how rude other drivers were, and he asked if she knew about a bakery that was only two blocks from her apartment. He had with him a freshly baked chocolate cake from the bakery, as well as the food from Joey's Diner.

The conversation continued as they ate, and it all felt so comfortable and natural to Beth. They conversed as if they'd known each other for much longer than they had, and she liked this fresh bond that they seemed to share.

After supper was polished off, along with a good amount of the cake, she watched as he unfolded the sofa bed, barely struggling with it. It usually took her a few good minutes to open it up for company. This man had skills that rippled through him with as much intensity as his muscles.

She began to grow tired as the conversation lulled off and Ray put on one of her slow jazz records. Before she was allowed to retreat to her bed, the doctor side of him reappeared. He checked her eyes with a tiny flashlight to look for dilation. Then, he checked her temperature to ensure she didn't have even a trace of a fever. When he was confident she was okay for the night, he helped her into bed and pulled a chair up to her bedside.

"Please tell me you're not going to read another dirty sex scene to me?" she asked him as she looked at him sleepily from her pillow.

"What? You didn't like it?"

"I liked it a little too much," she admitted. He smiled at her reply.

He leaned forward as if he was going to stand. Instead, he came in close to her and she thought he was going to kiss her. Readying herself, she pursed her lips and closed her eyes. Instead of his thick, scrumptious lips upon hers, she felt his hand on her cheek, double-checking for a fever. Disappointed, she opened her eyes and relaxed her readied lips.

"You're good to go," he said, withdrawing his hand and standing from the chair. "I'll check in on you in a few hours."

She smiled at him. "Good night, Doctor Ray."

He smiled back. "Good night, Patient Beth." Then, turning off her light, he left her to rest.

Drifting off to sleep, Beth readied herself for what promised to be sweet dreams.

* * * *

The next day, she was thankful she had help. She'd

expected to feel much better, but she instead experienced such an intense headache that it was crippling.

"I told you to take your meds," Ray said, giving her the medicine and ensuring she swallowed it down. "You don't want to have to stay at the hospital, do you?"

"No..." she muttered. He lifted her into his arms and carried her back to her bedroom.

"I know you woke up with energy, but you shouldn't have tried dancing in the living room." He laid her atop her bed and adjusted her pillow beneath her head.

"It came on so suddenly," she told him. The pills were taking effect. The headache was subsiding. "I feel beat now."

"You need to sleep," he said. She watched his face as his feet worked off his shoes. Then, fully surprising her, he climbed onto the bed and lay down beside her. "I'm going to make sure you rest if I have to stay right here beside you." He made himself comfortable and shut his eyes.

While blown away by this somewhat intimate moment, Beth smiled proudly to herself. Then, she snuggled in and relaxed. Tilting her head toward him, she looked at him... took in his resting expression. As coyly as she could, she sniffed his shoulder.

"Still got that cold?" he asked. With a jerk, Beth turned her head away.

"Yep," she replied and nearly chuckled from the moment.

Closing her eyes, she let the medication take over and slide her into an easy sleep.

* * * *

As medications usually made her do, she was in and out of sleep for most of the day, waking up for brief spurts to use the bathroom, eat, or grab water. Each time she awoke, Ray checked her vitals. He kept to his word and stayed with her the full day, with the exception of when she was in the bathroom. There, he gave her privacy. Otherwise, he sat with her, chatted with her, ate with her, and napped with her.

When she woke up the next morning, his arm was draped around her and he was spooning her, just as she had once hoped for. Like a true gentleman, he'd slept atop the covers and with his clothes on. Still, it made her feel both elated and secure. She'd never experienced a feeling like this before with any of the men she'd dated. It was why she chose not to date. Men were usually good for one thing and one thing only. This man, however, seemed incredibly different to her. He seemed like someone she could get used to being around.

Pulling out from his slumbering grip, Beth stood up and noticed she was neither dizzy nor had she a headache. The wound on her forehead was still sore, but otherwise, she felt pretty good. She decided she wasn't going to overdo it like she did yesterday.

No dancing around the living room like a fool. She'd take it nice and easy today, and maybe tomorrow, she could return to work.

That thought made her pause on her way to the bathroom. After two days of having her hero in her home, she wasn't sure she was ready for this experience to be over. If she was well enough to return to work, that meant his job here was done. Aside from that, he'd only taken three of his vacation days for this. He would be expected back at work tomorrow also.

Suddenly deflated, Beth completed her morning rituals in the bathroom and, despite his earlier warning of the drink, she brewed coffee. The fresh aroma helped perk her up, and the first sip aided in bringing her out of her newfound funk over work and wellness.

She was at the table and on her second cup when she heard Ray come out of the bedroom and enter into the bathroom, shutting the door behind him. A few moments later, she heard the toilet flush and water rush from the faucet. When he stepped from the bathroom, the first words out of his mouth were, "Is that coffee I smell?"

"Yep," she told him and smiled as he walked into the room. "And I don't care what you say. It's heavenly."

"I won't argue," he said and took a coffee mug from the cupboard, filling it. He blew on the brew to cool it a little and then sipped. A moan of pleasure left him as he savored the sip and swallowed it down. "Yep... that's good."

He sat across from her at the table and looked at her with pleasant but sleepy eyes and a slight smile on his face.

"What?" she asked as he eyed her.

"Just... enjoying you," he told her. His voice was silky smooth.

Beth blushed deeper. Averting her eyes from his, she looked at her coffee and watched the steam rise from it.

"How are you feeling?"

She looked at him again. "Pretty good," she said. "The wound is still sore on my forehead, but not as bad as it's been. No headache... no dizziness."

He nodded. "Good. As long as you're careful today, you should be ready for some normal activity tomorrow. You still can't go back to work until next week though."

Her eyes widened. She needed the income, even if she didn't want this time with Ray to come to an end. "I can't do that. I have to get back to work."

Ray shook his head. "No can do. Those work orders came from both of your employers. If you were to have another sudden headache like yesterday's... well, it's a chance they can't take. Legalities, you know."

"You told them about my headache?" she asked, hoping he hadn't. Wasn't there an oath of confidentiality that doctors took?

"Nope, but they each gave me possible scenarios that were incredibly close," he said. "I know times are tight and you need the money, but if you hurt yourself or make this worse, you could be out of work for a lot longer."

She knew he was right. She had to recover before she could do either of her jobs, but that didn't make things any easier. Now, she wouldn't have work to focus on when Ray left her tomorrow to return to the hospital. It would be business as usual for him, and she would be left alone at home with Elvis and *The Brady Bunch*.

It wasn't fair, and as she processed the news, she stood from the table and hunted for her cigarettes. She found a half a pack and her lighter on the kitchen counter, took one, and lit it. After a nice long drag, she looked back at Ray and said, "I guess it gives me time to clean out the closet and do some dusting." She blew out a puff of smoke. It slowly swirled through the space until it dissipated.

"You look a little deflated," he noted. "I thought you'd be happy to hear that your life can go back to a state of normal." He took a cigarette from the pack in his pocket and lit it. "That means you're healing. Come Monday, your whole world will be back to normal. Can't you enjoy a semi-normal state of life that doesn't include work, for just a few more days?"

She could, if it didn't mean she'd be broker than broke. Aside from that, she didn't want things to go back to even semi-normal if it meant he was leaving. That no longer seemed fair to her. Perhaps she was getting a little too attached, but she realized it and didn't care. She'd never met anyone like Ray before, and she didn't want to let him slip through her fingers.

Ashes fell from her cigarette to the floor and she realized she'd been ignoring it. Quickly, she took a drag, wishing it would calm her chaotic nerves.

"I suppose," she said, finally answering his question. "It's just… a curve ball. I wasn't expecting to be home that long."

He smiled at her and sipped his coffee. "It'll be okay. I'm sure you'll find some better ways to occupy your time than dusting and cleaning out your closet."

He chuckled, but she knew he was right. Looking at that handsome face that she'd grown used to so quickly, she could think of something much better than cleaning house that she'd like to do. Instead of voicing her thoughts, she said, "I suppose I could learn how to knit."

Ray laughed again. "Oh, come on now! What about your friends – Melanie and Dianna? You could hang out with them. I mean, they haven't been by once since I got here."

"It's because they know you're here," she replied without meaning to. Eagerly, she took another puff from her cigarette.

"What's that supposed to mean?" He eyeballed her and she thought he looked hurt or offended.

Deciding it was best to be straightforward with him, she elaborated. "They... think I might be trying to make a *play* on you, and they're keeping their distance." She snorted after her comment and reached for her coffee.

Now, Ray laughed more heartily. Beth eyed him, wondering what he found so funny about it.

"Well..." he asked when his laughter died down, "why haven't you?"

"Why haven't I what?"

"Made a move on me." His expression lightened and he smiled sweetly. "Heaven knows I've been hoping you would."

"Wait. What?" This was news to her. Aside from some vague flirting, he'd been a complete gentleman. "You were?"

He laughed again, this time much more lightly. For the first time since meeting him, Ray looked a little nervous and unsure of himself. "Yep. I mean... you're a beautiful woman, and I have to admit, I've enjoyed spending this time with you." His expression dazed and he looked lost for a moment. Then, he added, "After that kiss you gave me the other night – you know, after I risked life and limp to save you from danger... Well, you're all I can think about." He shrugged and smiled again. "Why do you think I *took* this home-care gig with you?"

She looked at him, blown away. "You've enjoyed checking my temperature and changing my bandage?"

"Yes!" he exclaimed and stood from his seat. "And everything else. I've enjoyed eating with you and talking with you, getting to know you and snuggling in the bed with you... I've been waiting for the right time to make a move on you, but I was hoping it would happen naturally."

Beth smiled as he approached her. She put her cigarette in the ashtray beside her. His joined it. With both hands, he pulled her close to him and looked deeply into her eyes.

Parting his luscious lips, he said, "You're a remarkable woman, Beth, and I can't imagine anyone being with you but me." Before she could reply, he kissed her – soft... tenderly – and closed the embrace around her, holding her to him. She fell into the kiss, enjoying its warmth, its passion, and its taste. She swore he tasted just as good as he smelled. And yes, in this heated moment of locked lips and the slight but delicious entanglement of their tongues, she smelled his scent all over him – that divine aroma that made her tingle in the most lustful of places.

Ray lifted her off her feet and she wrapped her legs around him. Still holding the kiss, he clumsily but safely carried her from the small half-kitchen, down the short hallway, and to the bedroom, where he lay her down.

With the kiss broken, he looked into her eyes and asked, "Do you want me?"

She studied him for a moment before replying, "More than

I've ever wanted anyone."

"Good," he said and nuzzled his nose to hers, "because I want you…" He kissed her again and whispered into her ear, "I have a surprise for you."

"A surprise?" she perked. She both loved and hated surprises but this sound like the type of one she would enjoy. "What surprise?"

He chuckled and cleared his voice. "This may have all been a little overly presumptuous of me, but while you were sleeping yesterday, I booked two tickets on a flight to New Orleans, hoping one of those tickets will be used by you. We leave first thing in the morning and fly back on Sunday."

She gasped and asked, "But I thought you had to go back to work tomorrow?"

"Vacation days, baby!" he exclaimed and kissed her again. Then, he added, "Besides, who better to look over you than a doctor? Not to mention, I can't have you just sitting here knitting and dusting and stuff. Since you can't go back to work, you might as well enjoy the time off."

It all seemed to fantastic and sudden to her, but she didn't care. Instead, she fell into the passion of Ray's kisses as they grazed her lips, chin and neck. Then, as he worked his way down to her chest and unbuttoned the top three buttons of her nightgown, she prepared herself for what she knew would be the greatest sex of her life.

"Are you sure you're up for this?" he asked her before they got too into it.

"I've been up for this since I caught you in the shower," she admitted. Then, with both hands, she pressed his head back to her flesh, eager for him to resume his talented kissing.

* * * *

They walked hand in hand down Bourbon Street, having just eaten lunch at the best little bistro. It was their third day in New Orleans, and they'd had the absolute best time. She'd forgotten her worries of work, leaving all real-life concerns back home where they belonged. She'd also mostly recovered from her accident. The sixty-nine on her forehead was still visible, but only barely. It was healing nicely. Still, she wore a wide-brimmed hat to help mask it. The bandage was no longer needed.

"Are you having a good time?" he asked her and gripped her hand as they walked.

"The best!" she told him excitedly. "I've always wanted to visit New Orleans, but I've never had the time or money to do it."

"Well, you're dating a *doctor* now," he said in a fanciful tone, "and doctors enjoy nothing more than spoiling their women."

"And just how many women are *you* planning on

spoiling?" she questioned, giving him a little side-eye.

"Just you, baby," he said and squeezed her hand again. "Just you."

She smiled again, having heard just the answer she'd wanted. She returned the squeeze and moved closer into him. Their hands separated and he wrapped an arm around her waist, holding her close as they walked.

'I can't *believe* we met Ray Charles today!" In her hand was a photograph of the performer that he'd graciously signed. "He has a pretty good signature for a blind guy."

Ray chuckled. "I'm pretty fond of his first name, myself," he joked.

A sudden breeze came by, gusting toward them and taking the photograph from Beth's hand, carrying it behind her.

"Oh, no!" she exclaimed and pulled out of Ray's grip. Turning around swiftly, she rushed after it and right into a lamppost, knocking her hat from her head and smacking hard against her forehead. "Well, crap…" she muttered and she looked Ray, who caught her as she began to faint.

"Here we go again," she heard him say as she fell unconscious.

The Scent of You

By

Kristi Ahlers

Chapter One

"You can do this, Arden. Millions of people fly every year; they arrive safely at their destinations. You're going to ovary up. When it's time to board, you'll find your seat, medicate your nervous backside and sleep until the plane touches down. You're not going to mentally flip out. You're not going to give into the anxiety clawing its way out of your belly. You're going to board this thing like you do it every day, with a smile on your face and an air of unperturbed class. This isn't a big deal." Arden muttered to herself as she made her way to the gate where her flight was departing from. "You'll go help your dumbass brother out of his jam…*again*…and come back home to the safety of your books, and fuzzy jammies."

With that mental and somewhat verbal pep talk she scanned the seating area for a place to park her butt until it was time to force herself into the flying metal tube of death…or the airplane as most referred to the hulking weighty thing outside the large floor to ceiling window. "Maybe I should medicate now," she said to herself as she looked at the full waiting area. There was not a seat to be found and decided she would go to the gift shop and buy a bottle of water—she'd read that it was best to drink just water on flights as it helped to counteract dehydration due to the dry recycled air in the plane, and help with tummy issues. Carbonation at thirty thousand feet doesn't react the same as it does on the surface of the planet. Who seriously needed a bloated and sore tummy when all one could use was a flying outhouse in the sky? She didn't do outhouses on the ground! Arden wasn't a math or physics person; she was a reading person. She was all about the books. Numbers, with letters, unless you're talking page numbers and letters forming sentences, was beyond her understanding. Who the heck cared what Y equaled? More like Y do you care? GAH!

She spun on her foot and spied a newsstand a few feet away, wandered into the shop and went to the cooler where five...yes, five different bottles of water were offered. Yeesh! She grabbed the cheapest, which was not saying much since the same bottle of water was four dollars cheaper outside the security area of the airport. She also snagged a bag of crackers, just in case her tummy decided it didn't care for being thirty million miles off planet earth, and made her way to the cashier.

She paid her eleven dollars for the snack size saltine crackers and small bottle of water and made her way back to the gate, where if possible, more people had managed to gather. Oh boy, with the weight of each human and their ridiculous bags beside more than half of them, plus the weight of the airplane, fuel, and bottles of miniature liquor, she began to wonder how on earth the plane would manage to get off the ground, let alone stay up in the air. Again, she recognized it was a math thingy and she didn't do math, because let's face it, this was stupid. The whole last forty-eight hours had been stupid. Once she finally got to New York, she was going to give her brother a stern talking to for putting her in this position. And maybe, just maybe, the return trip home would be done in a rental car. She'd always wanted to see the country; what better way to do it than in a sub-compact rental?

"Will *Horizon Air* passenger Arden Hillbrook please come to the podium at boarding gate twenty? Again, will *Horizon Air* passenger Arden Hillbrook, please come to the podium at boarding gate twenty?"

Arden swallowed hard, as she grasped her ticket and ID and made her way to the rather bored looking gate agent and tried to muster a smile. Difficult since Arden was wondering what fresh hell awaited her at the counter.

"Hi, I'm Arden Hillbrook." She hefted the strap of her canvas carryon further onto her shoulder and placed her ID and ticket in front of the agent. "Is there something wrong?" She nibbled on the inside of her cheek and prayed that everything was going to be okay. But, since the time her brother called her almost forty-eight hours ago in the middle of the night—nothing good ever comes from a phone call in the middle of the night—she seriously doubted this little interlude was going to net her something happy.

The gate agent offered a smile and looked at Arden's marked up boarding pass and ID before she turned her attention to the keyboard in front of her. "Unfortunately, this flight is over booked. We can either put you on a later flight, offer you a voucher, or we can move you to first class."

Arden frowned. "Wait, how do you move me to first class if the flight is overbooked?"

"Business class and main cabin are full; we have first class seats left available."

Arden contemplated taking the money and running but decided the better part of valor was to actually sort out her stupid brother, come back home and promise herself never to fly again. "I'll go ahead and take the first-class seat please." She handed over her boarding pass for the main cabin and smiled. "I guess something good is coming from this crummy trip after all."

"Not flying for pleasure, I take it?" the gate agent asked with a small smile.

"No."

In quick order, the agent printed off the new boarding pass and handed it over. "Well, I hope you manage to have some kind of fun while in New York."

"Thank you. I may actually take a day to see a few of the sights. I've never been there before. To be honest, the idea of that city intimidates me."

"Totally understandable! It's a big city and a lot of places aren't terribly brilliant. Just use your head and follow your gut."

"If I was going to do that, I wouldn't be getting ready to board a gas can with wings."

The gate agent laughed. "You're one of those, huh?"

"Terrified of flying?" Arden asked with a smile. "Why yes, yes I am. I'm thinking of setting myself up as president in a local chapter of *Oh heck no, I'm not flying!*"

The agent laughed again. "You'll be perfectly okay. I promise. If you'd like to step over to the forest green carpet, we will begin boarding first class in a few minutes."

Arden gripped her new boarding pass and smiled. "Thank you again."

"Enjoy your flight."

Arden stepped away from the counter, took a deep breath and made her way over to where the agent indicated. She took another deep breath to still the anxiousness taking over as each second of the clock ticked by that would lead her to walking down the jet bridge to the plane.

"I've got this. I can do this." She dug around in her carryon and pulled out one of her anxiety pills and cracked her overpriced water, took a sip and sighed.

"Good evening, ladies and gentlemen. We are going to begin our boarding processes and would like to ask you, in advance, to make quick work when stowing your carry-ons in the overhead compartment. Be mindful this is a full flight and smaller bags should be stowed under the seat in front of you. Thank you."

Arden gripped her canvas tote as if it were her lifeline to staying on the ground and closed her eyes, slowly took in a deep breath through her nose and let it out slowly through her mouth.

"Miss Hillbrook, we can let you board now," the gate agent came up to her and motioned towards the jet bridge.

Arden opened her eyes and noted she was the only one being escorted down the narrow space. Odd, she didn't realize that they boarded first class passengers one by one.

She walked down the sloping walkway towards the plane and her nerves gripped her in their sharp icy talons. "My brother is so dead meat when I get to him," she muttered to herself as she was met at the door of the plane by a smiling blonde flight attendant.

"Welcome aboard, Miss Hillbrook. The rest of the first-class cabin has been boarded. Please take your seat so we can close off the cabin from the rest of the plane before boarding of the main cabin takes place."

Hmmm, this was turning out to be odd, but whatever. Arden offered a shaky smile. "Thank you." She stepped into the galley area of the plane before the flight attendant indicated she turn to the left and move into the first-class cabin. Arden took one more deep breath and schooled her features into what she hoped was one of cool, calm confidence. She hoped it would indicate to her fellow passengers that this was an almost daily occurrence of jet-setting to big cities and not what was really going on in her head. She was mentally cursing—the only way she dropped the four-letter words most of society used as sentence fillers—as she stepped through the curtain. She looked up and stopped dead in her tracks. The small space was filled with the exception of two seats. The whole first-class cabin was filled with the members of the hottest rock band of the decade, *Sound Trigger*.

"Welcome aboard, darlin. You want to step into the lair here so the rest of the plane doesn't know we are on this flight?"

Arden looked up and then up again into the green eyes of Trig Martin, lead singer of her favorite band standing beside her by the curtain. "Oh, sorry. Yeah, uh…" She stepped forward, tripped and hit the floor with her knees and fell into the lap of Cade Montgomery, her favorite band member and the drummer. She groaned into his lap and wished for the world to swallow her whole. "I'm so going to kill my brother when I see him."

Chapter Two

"Well, that's the first time you've ever heard that with a woman's face near your junk huh, Cade?" laughed a deep voice behind Arden as an arm helped her up from the ground.

"God, I'm so, so sorry! I didn't mean to do that." She pushed her hair out of her eyes and was met with the smiling and beautifully deep blue eyes of Cade freaking Montgomery - the drummer for her favorite band, dude who played a staring roll in many a fantasy, and here she was literally falling face first into his lap. Up close and personal with the private parts of one of the sexiest men alive, according to a few magazines. The many ways she dreamed about getting a chance to meet this guy, let alone speak to him, but never did she think it would be like this. Like a twit who couldn't stay upright. Damn, she shouldn't have taken that anxiety pill before she got on the plane. No, she was so far from graceful and demonstrating calm sophistication, as if she met rock stars on the daily. None of her fantasies of meeting this band or this man included face planting into the very hard and surprisingly impressive lap of Cade Montgomery. "I hope I didn't hurt..." she waved in the general direction of his nether regions, "anything with my clumsy face plant." Arden squeezed her eyes closed. "Just shut up Arden," she muttered to herself.

"Are you okay, baby?" Cade reached out and brushed a strand of her hair back off her face. "No harm done to me, but that looked like a hard fall onto your knees."

"Yeah, no, I'm good." She wasn't good. She was mortified. She was horrified. She was...yeah, running out of words that rhymed with the previous words, because you know...life just loved to have a good laugh.

"Here...take a seat, sweets. Let's make sure you're okay," a new voice spoke over her.

She glanced over her shoulder, "Holy smokes! You're Killian! You play the guitar." She clapped her hand over her mouth before she said anything more uncool than she already had and dropped down into the seat across the aisle from Cade.

"Yes, yes I am and I do. And we have the pleasure of meeting...?"

"Arden. Arden Hillbrook." She held out her hand and took a deep breath – bad mistake as she inhaled a ton of masculine scents. Her mouth started to water, and she willed herself to lock her stuffing up and keep it together. Arden then took a moment to let her eyes settle on the rest of the men in the small space she now found herself. Cade now squatted beside her; Killian looked down at her and shook her offered hand. Julian, the band's bass player, offered a wink, and Trig smiled and crossed his arms over his chest.

Each one of these men grew more handsome than the last; there really wasn't a bad looking one in the bunch, but she was still partial to Cade. Which, in the grand scheme of things, really didn't matter. It wasn't like she was going to be spending time with these guys. Aside from the fact they were sharing a flight that is. She finally started to feel the effects of her pill and fatigue began to pull at her despite the excitement of the last few minutes. The sounds of the other passengers boarding the plane behind the curtain reached her ears and she realized she really needed to find her seat, sit down, find her Zen place and hopefully do this without catapulting herself into anyone else's personal space.

"I'm really, really sorry. I didn't mean to make a pest of myself." She stood, overwhelmed by the woodsy scent of Killian's aftershave, and the musky and spicy scent of Cade's beautiful self. "I'll..." she waved her hand, "find my seat and leave you guys alone. I mean you don't need me fangirling or doing anything stupid...or more stupid." She mentally slammed her hand over her mouth. "You know what? I'll just shut up and sit down." She looked down at her bag, which was now spilled all over the floor, and snatched up her ticket to see what seat she was supposed to be in. "Do y'all want me to sit somewhere in particular or the seat I was assigned?" She asked as she stuffed her belongings back into the tote, thankful that nothing embarrassing had flown out like her supply of feminine products.

Cade smiled. "Which seat were you assigned?"

She peered down at the ticket..." uh, row four A."

Cade held out his hand, "Please sit down in your seat, beautiful. Do you want anything to drink?"

"Uh, no. I read you shouldn't drink alcohol or bubbly stuff as altitude does something to your body and that stuff effects it differently. Plus I took my anxiety meds, so mixing that with a drink probably not a good idea." She smiled. "I mean, no one else here probably wants to see what would happen if my clumsy backside had liquor."

Trig leaned over and gazed at her butt and winked. "I don't see anything clumsy about you, Arden."

"Uh…thank you," she squeaked as she slid into the seat by the window. "Just…ah, ignore me and I'll leave you guys to do whatever it is you do when you fly. I promise to not take pictures or anything to sell to the paps. That's what you call the idiots that chase you with the cameras right?"

Killian out right laughed. "I love this girl!" he winked. They seemed to wink a lot. "We aren't worried about that, babe, I promise. And yes, the paps are vultures but part of the game we play in order to play our music."

"Gentlemen, we need you to take your seats so we can prepare the cabin for take-off," a member of the flight crew said as she gathered up the detritus of the pre take-off beverage service.

Arden nodded her head and settled in, pulling out her pillow, a small throw, her kindle to keep herself occupied provided she could forget she was hurtling above the earth at a million miles an hour across the sky. Once she was settled, she fastened her seatbelt low on her waist and made sure she triple-checked it was secure. She didn't want to go flying upward in case they hit turbulence, which, she knew they would once they flew over the Rockies. She actually dreaded that part of the flight. Correction, she dreaded this whole freaking experience and now instead of Joe Smith random stranger who would possibly lay witness to her flipping out a mile above earth, she had the hottest set of men in the world there to do it. Because, yeah, the universe was a bitch at times. She reached up and adjusted the air flow on her face, because she needed air badly and then sat back and realized she'd been watched the entire time by the Cade, Killian, Trig and Julian. Each wore their own sexy smile, with Cade flashing his dimples.

"Comfy, now, Darlin?" Trig asked as he leaned against the seats.

"As comfy as can be when one is sitting in a death trap," she muttered softly to herself before she screwed up a smile only to be met with male chuckles all around. *Crap! Was that out loud? Clearly it had been. When did I become such a verbal twit? Well, in for a penny at this point. After all, so far, I've face-planted in the crotch of my dream man, thrown my belongings all over the plane and found the inability to censor my mental ramblings. Yeah, my dumb brother is dead when I get to him.*

"Not much of a flier I take it?" Julian asked as he took the seat in front of her.

"Yeah, I try to avoid situations where I'm hurtling across the sky at light speed."

Cade sat beside her and settled down, fastening his own seatbelt before he reached over and pried her left hand out of the death grip it had on her right and ran his thumb over her knuckles. "Shhhh, it's going to be okay."

Arden wasn't aware she'd whimpered as the door to the cabin was closed.

"Ladies and gentlemen, welcome aboard *Horizon Air* flight 1543 with service to JFK. At this time, we ask all passengers to turn off and stow all electronic devices. Please make sure tray tables and seatbacks are in the upright position and all carryon items are stowed for take-off."

"Oh, God! I don't think I can do this." Arden shook her head and yanked her hand out of Cade's hold. For a brief moment, she allowed herself to sigh and then mentally kick her own ass for not taking time to appreciate the touch of the drummer she'd fantasized about for years. She really was a grade-A idiot. "I've got to get off this plane; my brother can pound sand. His drama, his problem. I mean I'm not his mom. Gah!" Her fingers were numb with panic and all she wanted to do was get off the plane, mentally kick her own ass for acting like a twit in front of her favorite band and then go home and lick her wounds. Then she could try to scrape together enough memories of the short time she'd been with the band for later when she was old and feeble. She could tell the tale of how she acted like a weirdo in front of famous people.

"Baby, shh." He reached over and refastened her seatbelt and drew her left hand back over to his side of the chair and rested it on his thigh. "I've got you."

"How's our girl?" Trig leaned over and looked at Arden.

Cade held her gaze and smiled. "She's going to be just fine."

Their words began to penetrate my muddled, anxiety riddled brain. *Their girl? Yeah, in what altered reality have I slipped into that the band I've been a fan of for years would be my seatmates on my trip to pull my dumbass older brother out of his own self-induced drama. That Cade Montgomery would be holding my hand against his thigh, a thigh that was very large and hard, and that my very lucky hand would be riding so close to his crotch I could reach out and stroke him. Not that I would. Hello! That would be totally out of line and assault since his being famous didn't give me carte blanche to do what I want when I wanted to with his person.*

Oh, but what I really want to do is to crawl over the arm rest of this seat, curl up in his arms and kiss him senseless. Oh God, that would be awesome...unless it wouldn't be awesome. The ability to bang away all sweaty and sexy on the drums and being a member of one of the hottest rock bands in decades doesn't mean he is going to be a good kisser. Maybe this was kinda like the old saying, don't meet your heroes as the expectation would or could be less, or at least something along those lines. It would be totally devastating if he kisses like a Saint Bernard all drooly and sloppy. Not that doggy kisses were bad, but still...dogs were not discriminating on where they put their tongues...

Male laughter filled the small space and Arden pulled herself out of her daydream.

"Well, I think I'm probably better at the whole sexing a woman up and being the best kisser out of this group," Killian stated with a smile. "I can honestly say none of the groupies Cade has kissed have compared him to a drooling Saint Bernard. But I can admit his mouth could be considered put in dodgy locations on occasion."

"Dude, shut the hell up! Like you've got room to talk," Julian teased from his seat. "I clearly remember a fan at the beginning of our career who was...let's just say...less than fresh and you seemed all in."

"That was a long time ago, I was under the influence of

Jack and since then I've been very discriminating on who I let near all this awesomeness."

Arden's face burned with humiliation and she tried to pull her hand away once again.

Cade just anchored her to him with a simple squeeze of his hand against hers. "You are adorable."

"I said all that out loud, didn't I? Could this flight get more embarrassing? I really shouldn't ask that. The universe has a tendency to say 'hold my karma' and dish out it's twisted form of humor."

She reluctantly pulled her gaze away from their clasped hands and met his dark blue gaze and her heart tripped around in her chest for a different reason. His dark hair, long enough to brush his shoulders, and his face was soft with concern and something else she didn't recognize given the fact she didn't know this guy at all. She pulled her lower lip with her teeth and tried for self-depreciation but simply didn't have the ability to pull that off so instead she went with honest. "I'm sorry. I know your seen as a body and not a person to a lot of people because of your music and that it's open season with touching you or assuming things, and I would never disrespect you or the other guys that way."

Cade leaned over and with his other hand traced his finger against her lower lip. Tingles of awareness rushed through her, leaving her feeling as if she'd stuck her finger in an electrical socket. Sadly, she knew exactly what that felt like thanks to her brother from when she was seven and he was eleven. He had her plug in a lamp that shouldn't have been plugged in thinking it would be funny. He was an ass but he felt bad after she was zapped and couldn't taste her favorite bologna sandwich for a few days, thanks to the jolt of electricity she'd been blasted with.

"You have nothing to apologize for, beautiful." He then leaned over and placed his mouth against hers. The touch was soft. He rubbed his lips slowly over her own and she about combusted from the heat of that simple but complex touch. He gently probed the seam of her lips with his tongue and she gasped at the sensation, and he slipped his tongue into her mouth. He tasted of mint and something smokey, and she relaxed into the kiss which was deep and wet and slow. It was a heartbreaking kiss. No urgency and not rushed. Instead, it was searching and learning, he licked at the roof of her mouth, his tongue danced along the sides of her cheek. She had no idea such a kiss existed or that she would ever experience it. Her tummy dipped and her heart tripped as he kept gently tormenting her mouth with his. She experienced that kiss everywhere.

Too soon, Cade pulled back and gently tucked a strand of her brown hair behind her ear and ran a thumb over her kiss-swollen lips. He bent and placed another kiss against her mouth and cupped her face with both of his hands. Hands that were large and warm. This kiss was just as gentle but shorter. Much shorter.

"I need to stop because you're not some groupie to be pawed at or taken in the lavatory."

"Uh?"

Cade smiled. "Where have you been all my life?"

"San Francisco?"

"My new favorite city."

The moment was interrupted when the flight crew went through their pre-flight survival lecture. *Okay, it was really just the safety demonstration, but I think my description is much more apt.*

Arden made sure she marked all the ways to get off the plane should all hell break loose and they survived the crash and when she was done doing that, she realized she was the entire focus of all four members of the band. Again.

"Yeah, we are going to have to keep her," Trig said as he winked.

"Yeah, I couldn't agree more." Cade smiled and kissed her once more. "I find I'm drawn to sunshine and cute. Who knew?"

Who knew indeed?

Chapter Three

The plane pushed back from the gate and Arden squeezed her eyes shut; she then prayed to whoever was listening that…

A) They didn't die

B) She didn't say anything stupider in front of hot dudes

C) She didn't get sick or freak out

D) See A.

Arden was relatively certain any great deity wasn't listening to her but it never hurt to try. Case in point, her mantra *please don't crash* was heard by Cade and Killian, who shared it with Trig and Julian.

"Flight attendants, please take your seat for take-off."

"Oh, good night nurse!" Arden moaned as the sound of the engines revving filled the space.

"Baby. Look at me." Cade gently touched her chin with his thumb and forefinger and turned her head, so she looked at him directly. "Okay, good. Now just focus on me and take a deep breath."

Arden did as she was told. She felt the plane rush the runway, she chewed on her lower lip and whimpered again, her stomach a mass of knots. "God, I think I'm going to be sick," she said.

"No, you aren't. You're fine. Just breathe with me, baby." Cade took a deep breath, held it and let it out again. Arden found herself mimicking him. "Good, girl." He brushed a finger down her cheek. "You've got this, sunshine."

"If you say so."

"I do."

At that moment, she felt the dipping sensation as the plane started to leave the ground and she squeezed her eyes shut, closing out the perfection of Cade.

She was about to give into her total fear and then it happened. Cade's soft lips were against hers once again. He held her still as he gently took her mouth, his tongue sweeping past her parted lips, and teased and tormented her own, licking and sucking gently until she melted into the kiss and started to kiss him back. She was kissing Cade Montgomery. He didn't kiss like a Saint Bernard. He kissed liked she'd always dreamed of being kissed. Soft and deep, gentle and fierce, claiming but soothing. Yes, all that happened with his mouth against hers.

Once again, all too soon, he pulled back, placing soft kisses on the corner of her mouth, her cheek and her forehead. "You did it, baby."

Arden looked around and blinked the fog of the kiss away and took stock of the fact that they were airborne, all alive and she once bloody again had the attention of all the guys. They all took time to smile at her. Cade took this time to take their connection one step further and folded the armrest up and pulled her up against him where he promptly made sure she settled in the crook of his arm. The spicy and musky scent of his skin filled her senses, and she buried her head in his t-shirt and took a deep inhale. Sandalwood and spice with a hint of mint. Whatever it was, whether his cologne or aftershave or just him, she didn't care. There was something so terribly soothing about it, she wanted to bottle it up and carry it with her for her return trip. Provided she survived this one, of course.

Cade ran his hand up and down her arm and he talked with his bandmates and occasionally placed a kiss on the crown of her head. She was perplexed by the actions of this drumming rock star. His seemingly strong attraction to her and the reaction of the rest of the group in general. The deep tone of his voice soothed her, and she curled tighter into his embrace and allowed her eyes to drift shut as she listened to them discuss their schedule the following day that was going to include three major interviews about their new album dropping and the tour getting ready to start there in NYC. Then they had meetings with their lawyer and record label. So, dudes were going to be busy. Arden could only imagine what it would be like to live life in the fast lane.

Yeah, she lived in the bay area but that was the extent of what she'd call excitement. She lived in a loft apartment above the little bookstore she owned. She barely made enough money to keep it open, but she couldn't bring herself to give up on it. Her beloved grandmother had started the bookstore, and it was the place Arden went after school and during vacations. She'd been a little girl who loved books, loved living in the make-believe world where heroes existed, girls could be heroes and romance and adventure were real things. As an adult, she continued to love fictional worlds where she could escape when things got to be too much. She could appreciate being able to travel to different times and historical locations and never leave the dubious safety of home.

Yes, it could be argued she didn't live life, she read about it, but she didn't think that was such a horrible thing. After all, she did have friends and she went out and had fun, even though she would never, in any way, be considered a party girl. Her idea of a great date would be dinner and cuddling on the sofa with whatever must-watch series on *Netflix* or *Hulu* was on at the time. She didn't need expensive dinners or gifts or exotic locations to be happy. Simple made her happy. A warm cup of tea and a good book. Laughing with friends until you're crying and your tummy hurt. The idea of living like Cade and the rest of the band seemed odd to her. Scary.

Eventually, her mental musing and Cade's deep voice lulled her to sleep. She didn't know how long she slept before all hell broke loose and she catapulted up out of her seat.

"Easy there, tiger." Trig placed a hand on her arm and pulled her back into his arms. "It's just turbulence. You're okay.

Arden looked wildly around. "Where is Cade?"

"He had to use the lav. He'll be right back."

"But…he should be belted down. He could get hurt!"

"Easy, Arden. This is light chop; he will be back in a second." This was said by Killian.

"Light chop? *Light chop?* Are you *insane*?" Her question was answered by the plane dropping what felt like four thousand feet and a less than lady-like screech slipped past her lips. "Oh, God! Someone go check and make sure he's not passed out on the floor the bathroom. Oh, God! Those floors are so dirty!"

Trig kissed her temple and stood. Before she could tell the guys to quit smiling like loons and go make sure their friend and bandmate wasn't knocked out on the filthy lavatory floor with a brain injury and a possible need for a tetanus shot, the comforting scent of Cade surrounded her as he slid into his seat. "Hey, I'm okay, baby. Shhh." He wiped a tear off her cheek. "Sweetheart, you're breaking my heart." She gave a glad cry and wrapped her arms around his neck, strangling him as she clambered into his lap.

"Oh, God! You're ok!"

"Yeah, babe, I'm fine." He kissed her forehead and jostled her, so they were both belted in and he still maintained his hold on her. "It's just a little turbulence."

"I…I know."

"Think of this as potholes in the sky. Planes aren't pulled from the air to crash to the ground with turbulence, I promise," Killian said with a gentle smile.

"How do you know so much about that?"

"I actually have a pilot's license."

"You know how to fly? On *purpose*?"

Killian laughed. "Yeah, I do."

"Huh, who knew?" Arden muttered as she tried to still her frantic breathing.

"We're crossing over the Rockies. Once we get to the other side, it should smooth out. The pilots right now are probably trying to find smooth air as we speak. I promise, you'll be okay."

"Thanks, Kill." Arden yawned. She was so tired. It took a lot out of a girl to fangirl *and* flip out over flying. Dual tasking at its best. Plus, she'd had her medication, which normally really made her sleepy. She would offer her kingdom for a flat surface that wasn't moving so she could sleep without fear of some horrifying fiery crash.

"Anytime, Arden. Sleep. The flight will pass quicker."

"I would if I could." Another yawn slipped passed her lips.

Cade shifted her so she could still wear her seatbelt and lay her head in his lap. Since she was all of five-one, her shortness allowed for her to curl up in a ball. Julian leaned over the seat and covered her with her blanket and Cade started to run his fingers through her hair. With the soothing action and the scent of Cade filling her senses, she once again drifted off, this time into a dream free sleep.

* * * *

Cade leaned his head back against his seat and pondered the shift his world had taken in the last few hours. The small woman curled up in his lap was the catalyst of this shift and he normally would've gone running from any kind of commitment in the past, choosing to live his life and enjoy the rock-n-roll lifestyle he'd been embracing for the last five years. But somewhere along the line, it wasn't as fulfilling as it had been, and he'd been hard pressed to say why. The 'why' was he didn't have an Arden. This person he knew nothing about. Well, he knew she had the propensity to speak her mental musings, which was adorable and hilarious at the same time; she had a rabid fear of flying that broke his heart, and she had a loyalty streak that ran deep that pushed her to get on a plane to help her brother despite her fear of flying. What his problem was, he didn't know, but it impressed the hell out of him that Arden apparently loved her brother deeply enough she put her own fears aside to help him.

"You're so not letting her go, are you?" Trig asked on a whisper as he smiled and nodded to Arden.

"Not at all."

"Good. I haven't seen you this relaxed since...ever."

Cade looked at his best friend. "I haven't felt this relaxed since ever."

Julian stood between the two and looked down at Arden. "We will need to do something about her anxiety. We can't take buses everywhere, but I'm down to make sure the label schedules our gigs with enough time to travel via the road when we can."

The fact that Killian and Trig nodded in agreement warmed Cade's heart. In the beginning, buses were all they could afford when it came to touring. The bigger the venues, the more money, the easier travel came until they had their own jet and literally jetted where they wanted and when. They'd have been on said jet if it hadn't been in for maintenance and the need to get to New York tomorrow. Everything happened for a reason and Cade knew the reason they had to bogart the first-class section of this flight was curled up in his lap. Provenience actually.

"I'm going to need paper and pen ASAP." Cade wrote most of their songs and had been in a slump but one tiny little miracle with big brown eyes, and a mouth that begged to be kissed inspired him. Had someone asked him if he'd believed in love at first sight four hours ago, he'd have laughed his ass off. But truth was, he'd found his forever with a face-plant in his lap and a kiss.

"You got it." Killian went to the overhead and pulled down a notebook and pen and handed it to Cade.

Cade smiled. "How fast do you think we can write and compose a song?"

Trig laughed softly. "In enough time to perform it in three days and woo the girl."

"I was hoping that would be the answer." Cade smiled and, with care, lowered the tray table, making sure not to disturb Arden and began scribbling away.

Chapter Four

Life, Arden knew, was really just a series of moments that, when compiled together, formed a story. Everyone lived a story. Some happy, some sad, some tragic and some just darn right boring. Arden didn't realize her life had been the last on that list until she boarded a plane headed east and fell into the lap of who she thought would be the love of her life, if…

 A) Life was a Hollywood movie, and the dorky girl gets the hot rocker

 B) Said hot rocker would choose her when he could have anyone (think models, of course)

 C) She was sophisticated and brave enough to say something regarding her unprecedented feelings.

 D) Said rocker could read minds and she wouldn't have to embarrass herself and say anything.

 E) See C.

Yeah, so here I am waking up with drool on my cheek, the warm scent of coffee filling my senses and the terrifying fear this has all been a dream and I didn't meet my favorite band. Didn't kiss Cade Montgomery more than once and didn't fall asleep with his arms around me and his scent comforting. And that if it weren't all a dream, the fear that all the emotions were one-sided and he doesn't feel the same way as I do and I'll never have this time with him again. Okay, you needed to be real, Arden. He isn't in love with you. You aren't ever going to see him again in person once they walked off the plane and this isn't going to be your life defining moment where you experience your heart literally walking away from you. Yup, when I get home, I'll get right on adopting all those cats—which I hope won't dine on me once I die alone surrounded by cat trees, catnip and grains of litter all over the floors and 'what could've been' regrets.

"Cats huh?"

"For the love of… I need to sew my damn lips shut. You heard none of that. Capisce?"

Killian laughed. "I don't suggest sewing lips shut. That's just too much crypt keeper horror for me and I heard nothing."

"Smart man." Arden sat up. "Sorry I drooled on your jeans." She wiped her cheek and once again lamented that the god or goddess didn't grant her *any* of her requests on this trip.

"No worries. I've had much worse on my jeans, trust me."

Arden shivered. "I don't even want to know." She bent over and retrieved her bag and pulled out her hairbrush. She made quick work of brushing out the tangles and scraped it back into a high ponytail. She then rummaged around for a breath mint because, eew, flight breath, and tried to pretend waking up on a plane surrounded by rock stars she just met but felt she knew was a normal everyday thing.

"So how long are you going to be in New York?" Killian asked as he stretched his legs out.

Arden looked around for Cade and saw him in a deep conversation with Trig. As if he sensed her gaze, he looked up and smiled and winked. "Hey, beautiful, how are you feeling?"

"I'm good."

"I'll be over there in a second, okay?"

"Yeah, sure, take your time. I got this."

"Yeah, you do."

"So, you gonna answer me or what?" Killian asked as he tugged on her ponytail.

"Uh, well I'm supposed to climb on another plane in four days…provided I don't just give in to doing a cross country road trip home."

"Four days. Nice. Plenty of time."

"Time for what?" Arden asked.

"For you to do whatever it is you have to do."

"Oh…yeah. One can hope anyhow. My brother apparently has a first world problem that now needs to be my problem. So hopefully I can help him sort it out in four days."

Killian laughed. "Do we know what this problem is?"

"No clue. Just that I needed to get my ass to New York sooner rather than later because he needed me."

"Hmm, not cryptic at all."

"That's Mitch. One would think he had the ovaries what with the drama he brings to life. Not that drama is an ovary only problem. Gah, I'm being sexist, but you understand."

"Yeah, babe I do." Killian winked and stood.

"You keeping my girl company, Kill?"

"More like she's entertaining me."

Cade smiled and dropped down in the seat Killian vacated. "So, baby, we're going to be landing in less than an hour."

Arden smiled. Or at least she hoped it was a smile. Landings were dangerous and she was afraid of that. But, the thing that scared her more was the idea of getting off this plane and going away from Cade and the guys. In a very short time, they'd become very important to her. "I know."

"So, we have a lot that needs to happen before we land."

"What?"

"Well, I need to know a few things."

"Such as?" Arden was thoroughly confused. "I mean I promise I won't divulge anything about y'all being on the plane or any of the conversations we had. And I swear I didn't sneak any pictures."

Cade leaned over and kissed her forehead. "Not what I was worried about, babe."

"Oh. Okay?"

"Yeah, so I need to know what your favorite color is, your favorite food. I already know you're terrified of flying, but what makes you super happy? I want to know if you prefer cats to dogs.

"I have it on good authority she is a cat person." Killian answered as he took his seat.

Arden narrowed her eyes at him and drew her finger across her neck in the internationally known symbol of slashing a throat.

Cade watched this and laughed "I feel I'm missing something."

"Not at all."

"Dude, you have no idea."

Arden leaned forward and hissed, "You're off my Christmas card list now, buddy. Tread careful."

Cade outright laughed again, and he was joined by Trig and Julian this time.

Arden met his gaze. "You were saying?"

"Oh, yeah, okay, where was I?"

"If she liked cats or dogs," Julian supplied helpfully.

"I like hamsters." Arden didn't know if she hated or liked hamsters, but she wanted to get off the topic of pets like yesterday as she didn't need help from Killian to make her look like a dork. She did that fine all on her own, thank you very much.

"Babe, you so don't like hamsters. And I have to do the research on if they eat the dead." Killian winked.

"That's it. No Christmas card or homemade baked goodies for you!"

"Oh, crap! You do realize that he doesn't speak for the group right, Arden?" Julian asked as he sat down and fastened his seatbelt. "I'm all about homemade cookies. My favorite is the rolled out frosted sugar cookies." He rubbed his stomach. "Those are the shit!"

"Duly noted." Arden smiled.

"Hello? Do you idiots mind? I'm trying to get to know my girl in the little time we have left on this flight."

Arden looked out the window and noted that they were indeed coming out of the clouds and flying over the city. She took a moment to gasp at the vastness of this huge city and started to get a little nervous since

A) She'd never been to New York City

B) She didn't know what fresh hell awaited her with her brother

C) Suddenly being on an airplane wasn't that horrible because of Cade

D) She'd have to walk away from Cade and the rest of the guys and that really hurt more than it should.

E) See D.

Cade grabbed her hand and gave it a squeeze. "Are you okay, Arden?"

"What?" She turned back to him. "Oh, yeah, uh, sure. I've just never been to New York and I didn't realize how big it was."

"Ladies and gentlemen, we have begun our final descent into New York City. We ask at this time to turn off all electronic devices and stow away all carry-ons. The flight crew will come through the cabin one last time to pick up anything you'd like to discard before landing."

Arden's heart started to trip around in her chest. "Oh goodie, the controlled crash of the program."

"Hey, great description!" Killian smiled as he sat down and fastened his seatbelt. "You're actually not wrong about that."

"Will you shut the hell up, Kill?" Cade asked as he smoothed his thumb over Arden's knuckles.

Arden smiled at the man beside her. The man who managed to become so very important to her in less than eight hours. A man she was going to have to walk away from. Her throat tightened but she refused to cry.

"So, what's your favorite color," Cade asked as he soothed her with his attentions.

"Purple."

"Favorite food?"

"Depends on the moment. I love sushi. Anything with lobster in it. Hmmm, brie cheese, but it has to be melted and super gooey. I love a good burger but it has to be good, not some chain restaurant's idea of a burger."

"Nice." Cade smiled. "What is your favorite season?"

"I guess I like paprika if it's not used too much. Does vanilla count as a spice? I really love vanilla. I have to admit I'm not a spicy spice kinda girl."

The guys all laughed softly.

"No, baby, what season like spring or summer." Cade brushed a strand of hair off her face.

Arden willed the world to just open up and swallow her. Of course that's what he meant. Because who talks about spices in a kitchen cabinet as a form of getting to know a person. Unless, of course, they were talking to a chef, which, she wasn't. Yeah, she was a bright one all right.

"Hey, did we lose you?" Cade asked.

"No, I couldn't be that lucky after being such a dork."

"Hey, none of that. Easy mistake. So…what's your favorite season?"

"Fall! I love the fall. I love Halloween. Best holiday ever!"

"Agreed. What is your favorite book?"

"Well, as far as classics go, I love Les Miserable. And of course, Jane Austen. I love romance in general and I find that I'm also learning to like fantasy fiction, although, don't tell anyone…I'm not a fan of *Lord of the Rings*. I know, blasphemy, but it is what it is."

"That's it, Cade! You need to drop the dead weight of Arden. Who doesn't love *LOTR*?" Trig asked in mock horror his quick smile easing his words.

"I know, I know, but to me it just doesn't entertain. I mean, who needs to read fifteen pages describing a hole in the ground. I mean while I'm at it I also loath *The Wizard of Oz*," Arden said with a shrug.

"When is your birthday?"

"December eleventh."

"Cookies or cake?"

"Wedge of melted brie and a French baguette. I'm not a huge fan of sweets, although, I'll kill for a good French Macaron. And I loathe ice cream, before you ask."

Cade smiled. "Welcome to New York, beautiful." He kissed her softly on her mouth.

Arden was so invested in answering all his getting-to-know-her questions, wondering why he was even bothering as she wasn't a person someone like him would normally pay attention to, that she paid zero mind to the plane's descent and finally landing.

"Thank you." Tears burned the back of her eyes. She now knew why he asked the questions and she kissed him back softly. "You made this horrible flight not horrible."

A flight attendant came up to the guys. "The door is open, and they are ready for you to deplane. The limo is already planeside."

The guys stood and gathered their things. Cade held his hand out. "Come with us?"

"Oh, I can't do that!"

"Yes, you can. We want you to. We can drop you off where you're going on our way to the interviews we have this morning. Besides, I'm not quite ready to say goodbye to you yet."

"Come on, Arden. Let us take you into New York City, Rockstar style!" Julian winked as he grabbed her blanket and kindle. The guy really did have a long arm reach.

"Okay, if you're sure it's all right. I don't want to be a leech."

"Baby, its more than all right. It's perfect." Cade kissed her cheek and held out his hand. "Come on, let's get out of here."

And that's how Arden Hillbrook made her first trip to New York. First class all the way, with the hottest males on the planet. Not bad for a first time doing something.

Chapter Five

Arden gave Cade her brother's address, and they made their way into the city. She knew this was stupid. She should've just stayed on the plane, gotten off like the rest of the passengers, taken a cab into the city. But no. She wanted to delay the inevitable because she was twisted that way. Instead, she sat in the back of a limo—something everyone should be able to experience at least once in their lives—in between Cade and Trig and she wished the drive would last forever. But it didn't and soon she was in front of her brother's brownstone. "Thank you very much for everything. It was beyond great meeting you all." She smiled as she grabbed her tote.

Leaving Cade and the guys was proving to be heartbreaking, which was stupid. She really didn't know these guys beyond the superficial and not really in that way either. She knew them as well as anyone else who had never met them. Well, with the exception of Cade. Cade, she knew what he felt like and smelled like and even tasted like. All those things she imprinted into her memory for when she was alone and missing him. Which again was stupid. He'd drop her off and probably forget about her in a day. Hello…he was a busy rock star.

"Hey, wait." Julian stopped her with a hand on her arm.

"You're not getting away that easy." He leaned over and kissed her on the forehead. "It was a pleasure to get to meet you."

"Thanks," Arden said as she squeezed his hand.

"Where is my kiss?" Killian leaned over and placed a big loud smacking kiss on her mouth. "You may be Cade's, but I reserve the right to take his place should he screw up."

"Oh, I'm not Cade's." Arden blushed. "But, thank you."

"Uh, you are too his. Are you kidding me?" Killian frowned. "Even now he's trying to hold back punching me in the face for stealing a kiss."

"You're ridiculous and you're still on my not getting a Christmas card list." Arden teased.

"You wound me, sunshine. You cut deep." He placed a hand dramatically over his heart and flopped back against the leather seat.

Arden couldn't help it; she giggled. He was a total clown and she loved him for that.

Trig leaned over and kissed her cheek. "See you on the flip side, sweets."

"See you." Arden slid out of the limo and onto the street. She managed to grab her bag and then Cade was standing beside her.

"Give me your phone."

Arden handed her smartphone over and frowned. "I don't

need a selfie with you."

Cade smiled. "Is that so?" He typed away on her phone and then pulled her close, held the phone out and said, "Smile."

Arden smiled and before she knew it, Cade placed his mouth over hers and kissed her. Then he sent the picture to himself. "I'm going to call you after I'm done with our interviews today. You are going to answer, and we are going to talk. This between us isn't over, baby. It's the start of something amazing."

Cade held out Arden's phone and she took it, stunned by what he said, what this meant and the utter certainty she probably wasn't cut out for any of it. "Cade…"

"Baby, I don't have a lot of time, but you need to know that I'm a whole lot crazy about you. You make things so much better than they were and I'm not letting you go. I know you don't think you're going to fit with my lifestyle or my life, but you're wrong; you will. You just have to be willing to take a chance. Give us a chance. I'll prove to you this isn't a joke and that I'm serious. Watch our interview today okay? Promise me?"

"Okay, I promise." She offered a shaky smile.

"Good. Now, kiss me like you mean it."

So saying, Cade placed his mouth against hers and hauled her up against him. He wrapped one arm around her lower back while the other hand cupped her face so gently it brought a tightness to her throat. He kissed her deeply, his tongue sliding against hers, sipping and nipping, teasing and claiming. It was everything a perfect kiss should be, and Arden was getting it from a famous rock star on the sidewalk of a busy New York City street. If this is was what being claimed publicly was like, she was all about that. Cade pulled back and pulled her forehead to his mouth and he placed a hard kiss there. "I'll call you. Answer the phone, baby."

"I will." She watched as he slipped back into the limo and the door closed. Then, the car pulled out into the flow of traffic and Arden turned, walked into the building with four thoughts on her mind:

A) She was going to hug her brother and thank him for his drama, as that drama brough Cade into her life.

B) She was going to fix his problem, watch an interview and try not to freak out about the radical change her life just took.

C) Pray that Cade wasn't just saying things because she was a novelty.

D) Pray Cade would keep his word and call.

* * * *

Cade stepped out of the green room and made his way towards the soundstage where they were going to do the last of the three interviews they'd been signed up for…that day. He was tired, and they still had to hit the studio for a few hours later in the afternoon. That was the thing about dropping new albums and starting new world tours – you had to do a lot of talking about it when they really just wanted to get in some practice time, take a shower, eat and sleep for a few hours.

"Are you really going to do what you said you're going to do?" Killian asked as they dodged people in the hallway while heading towards the set. "Make sure you're really serious, dude. We all love her, and we don't want her to get hurt."

Cade stopped dead in his tracks and turned to see his best friends, all wearing smiles but also looks of concern. Yeah, he was about to dive into the deep end with this announcement. Hell, he wasn't even one hundred percent sure she felt the same way, but that's why they called it wooing and if he misread the signs and she didn't feel the same way, well, then Cade would experience his first true heartbreak and he'd learn to deal. He'd fallen in love at thirty thousand feet in the air with a beautiful, bookish woman who embraced the simplicity of life, loved to read, was funny as hell and kissed him back in a way he'd never been kissed. In fact, they'd only kissed with no rush to bed, no groping, no sex and he was all in. Like, sign him up, he'd marry her today all in. "I know you all think I'm insane, but I love her. Not that I *think* I'm in love; I know I am. I can't imagine another day going by without her in it. I can't imagine not hearing her voice or seeing her smile. I can't imagine going to bed tonight and her not being in my arms.

"Jesus, you're serious," Julian stated as he nodded his head. "I approve, dude. She's awesome. And we love her too. Just know that as much as we love you, you hurt her, and you'll answer to us."

"Wouldn't have it any other way."

"Okay, let's go announce the album and get you the girl." Trig slapped him on the back, and they all made their way to the set of seats they were to occupy for the last interview.

Chapter Six

"Your big first world problem was you're getting married?" Arden stood there dumbfounded. "You didn't even tell me you were dating anyone."

"I know, Ari but when you know, you know. You know?"

Yeah, she knew all right. Case in point: she took a flight, fell in love and did that all in less than eight hours. The fact she was in love with a famous person added a new level of angst to the situation. Oh, and the fact she wasn't one hundred percent sure he felt the same way kinda sucked. But, on the other hand, he kissed her right on the streets of New York City, where anyone could see them, and he didn't seem to give a crap. So, there was that. But, yeah, she was going to keep this all on the DL until she had confirmation things were the same for Cade. The fact they had been apart for only a few hours and she was missing him like they'd been apart for a week or longer was disconcerting, but it was what it was and she couldn't do anything about it at this point.

"So, when is the wedding?"

"Tomorrow."

"Tomorrow, as in like…"

"Tomorrow, yes, Ari."

"Uh. Okay, so no huge problem that needs to be solved."

"No. Just you as my only family member there with me when I marry Claudia. You're going to love her by the way. She's awesome."

"I'm sure I will. I'm super happy for you." Arden dropped down onto the sofa and rested her head back against the cushion. "I'm so tired."

"Sleep, dork."

"No, dude that will make the jetlag worse or so…"

"You've read." Mitch laughed.

Before she could respond, her phone dinged.

Cade: Turn the television to channel 4 now!

"Hey, where is your remote?"

"On the coffee table. You want to watch *Netflix* and chill or what?"

"No, I need to turn it to channel 4."

Mitch came over and turned on the television and dropped down beside her. "Have a burning desire to watch a morning show? Did you bump your head? You hate stuff like that."

"No, I didn't bump my head. Now Shhh."

"Welcome back, New York City. As promised, we are now joined by one of today's hottest rock bands, *Sound Trigger*. They are getting ready to embark on a world tour in a few weeks and are joining us today to talk about their new album, and the tour. Welcome, guys."

"Hello, Maryanne." Trig smiled. "Thanks for having us."

"So, a new album, a new tour…do you guys ever stop?"

"No. You stop, you lose the momentum. Music is a live thing, and it needs to be fed and nurtured," Julian said with a smile. "It can be tedious and tiring but you never know when something awesome is going to come your way, or what will inspire you."

"Cade, it's been said that you do the majority of the writing for the band. What is your process?"

"I love to tell a good story, that is what songwriting is all about. Normally you write about what you know, or what you experience."

"Your band isn't really known for its power ballads. Is there a reason for that?"

"Actually, up until today, I never had the desire or the inspiration to write a love song, or power ballad, as you call it."

"I take it that's all changed for you?"

"Yeah, you could say that."

Arden's heart stuttered in her chest. God, he was beautiful. His dark hair brushed his shoulders, the tight black t-shirt hinted at the defined wall of muscle that made up his chest and abs that she'd felt but yet hadn't seen in person. She also hadn't seen the ink that danced up his corded arms in person either, but she noted the ink now and had the overwhelming desire to trace the pattern with her mouth. What on earth was wrong with her?

"Are you saying the hottest drummer in rock'n'roll is taken?"

"I'm really hoping so."

Arden sat up and blinked.

"You hope so?"

"Yeah. I mean. I know how I feel. I'm just hoping Arden feels the same way."

Arden covered her mouth with her hand as the meaning behind his words filled her heart. This beautiful man was putting himself out there on national television without any real indication that she cared the same way to prove he was serious. That this was real for him.

"She's a lucky woman."

"No, I'm going to be the lucky one if she feels half of what I feel for her."

Mitch looked at her dumbfounded as Arden fumbled for her phone and pulled up his text. She knew Cade wouldn't get it now, they were doing a live interview, but he'd have her response when he was done.

Arden: Is it too soon to tell you I love you?

This was a bold move on her part, but the emotion was what she felt. She loved this guy, as crazy as it was. He soothed her and made her happy, made her feel safe, and she wanted to be those things for him. So, without further thought she hit send.

"Is there something you want to tell me, little sis?"

"Yeah, I fell in love on a plane last night."

"With Cade Montgomery of *Sound Trigger*."

"Yup, with Cade Montgomery."

She watched as the guys talked and then in dumbfounded disbelief watched as Cade pulled his cellphone out of his pocket - on live television - and read her text. The smile that spread across his face was beautiful and she knew they were destined for each other.

"No, baby, it's not too soon. Love you too," He said, for all the world to hear.

Never in her wildest dreams did she think she'd hear Cade tell her he loved her, let alone have the first time he said it where millions could hear it.

"So, your lady feels the same?"

"Yeah, she does. My world just got one hundred percent happier." He winked at the camera and blew her a kiss. "That will have to do until I'm done, babe."

Holy! Crap!

Chapter Seven

Arden paced and then sat down, got up and paced again while she waited for Cade to knock on her brother's door. He'd called her the minute he was done with the interview and told her he was on his way and to not move. Well, there you go. He was really all in. He was really going to see this through. Arden managed to somehow capture the attention and love of Cade Montgomery.

The knock at the door filled the space and Mitch smiled and walked over to the entrance, grabbing his coat on his way. He opened the heavy wooden door and stepped aside to let Cade enter. Before Arden could say anything, Mitch did.

"Nice to meet you. I'm Mitch, Arden's older brother. Hurt her and there will be no where you can run that I won't find you." He smiled at Arden. "I'm going to meet Claudia and her family for dinner. I'll see you tomorrow. Don't forget, wedding at one."

"I won't forget."

Mitch walked out the door, leaving Cade and Arden alone. Suddenly, she was overcome with doubt and fear and…yeah, doubt.

"Stop, beautiful. I can see the wheels of your mind running a million miles an hour. We will take this as fast or as slow as we need to. But know you are mine, and we are going to make this work, because last night marked the first night you slept in my arms and the last night I won't have you by my side, if I can help it."

"I'm a weirdo who loves to read, speaks her internal thoughts out loud, is terrified of flying, and of cotton balls - they squeak when you touch them. They give me chills. But not in a good way. I'm not a world class traveler, I have no idea how I'm going to react when my face is plastered all over social media. I mean, I'm not model skinny and I never will be."

Cade closed the distance between them and silenced her litany with a kiss. A kiss she felt everywhere. When he pulled back, she whimpered. She wanted more, she wanted him to make love to her, claim her totally as she claimed him back. "I love you're not model skinny. You're real and sweet. You make me laugh and make me feel one hundred feet tall. You're not impressed with the rock star wrapping. You see *me*. That's priceless, baby. We will deal with the paps. I'm not saying it will be easy, or smooth sailing all the time, but life isn't smooth sailing or happy all the time anyhow. That's what makes the ride worth taking. Take the ride with me, Arden. Please."

Arden smiled and wrapped her arms around his waist. "I'll take any ride, even one on a plane, if you're there to hold me, where I can smell your skin and know I'm loved and protected."

"Always, baby. Always."

* * * *

Two days later, Arden was standing backstage as her boyfriend pounded away on the drums while the band killed it on their latest single. If someone said before she boarded the flight in San Francisco that four days later this would be her reality, she would've had a good belly laugh. She wasn't laughing right now. She was dancing and singing and living her best life.

Now, this wasn't to say there wasn't a lot that needed to be addressed. There was. She wasn't going to be able to join them on tour right away because hello...she had a bookstore to run, or find someone to help her run. She lived in the Bay Area; the guys were based out of Chicago. There were a lot of logistics that needed to be sorted and they would be...eventually. In the meantime, she was going to live life instead of reading about it because...

    A) She'd met the love of her life and the world was hers for the taking.

    B) Fear was only something if you dealt with it alone. She now had Cade and three new older brothers to look out for her in the form of Trig, Killian and Julian.

    C) See A.

DCL Publications, LLC

http://www.thedarkcastlelords.net

Find our books at any fine online retailer.